rest area

stories

stories

Clay McLeod Chapman

 n e w
y o r k

LIBRARY OF CONGRESS CATALOGING-IN-PUBLICATION DATA

Chapman, Clay McLeod.
Rest area : stories / by Clay McLeod Chapman.—1st ed.
p. cm.
ISBN 0-7868-6737-X
1. Domestic fiction, American.   2. Horror tales,
American.   I./ Title.
PS3603.H36 R47 2001
813'.6—dc21   2001016659

Book design by Richard Oriolo

FIRST EDITION

10   9   8   7   6   5   4   3   2   1

for all my fathers,
D.C., H.M., W.H., J.C.

contents

rest area

stories

rest area

Carolina plates. You guys have come far. Where you
heading? Out Midwest? Lord, that's a long haul. You've got
to be nomadic to drive all that way, nowadays.

Beats flying, that's right. The only way to travel, if
you're pining for the sights. And with the whole family, boy.
Who's the little tinker in the backseat? Hi there. She doesn't
mind being buckled up all day? Good for her. My daughter
and I did our own bit of venturing cross-country this summer,

just the two of us. I took off from work, rented a car. We ambled along the back roads for weeks.

Could you tell me if you've seen her? Here. Here's a photograph of her. Well, a photocopy of her. You can't make out her features very well. It's not really her face anymore— shades from it. But if you look here, right above the smudge, you can still spot her smile. Her teeth are in there somewhere. You just have to fix your eyes on it for a while. They'll rise up to you, if you squint hard enough.

That's Grace's smile.

I'm pasting them up all along here. On the soda machines. There's a whole stack with the tourist pamphlets. Just in case someone's seen her. Can't be too sure, now.

You didn't, did you? Did you see a girl on the road? Red hair. Cream shorts. A cherry on vanilla.

No sign of her? No.

We drove through here a few months ago, about halfway into our trip. The A/C was on its own time, leaving us with the windows down for most of the ride. The heat wasn't the problem, really. I could've dealt with that. It's the puddle of sweat forming at the stem of your neck that drowns your temper. The wet itch you get all along your scalp. Let your nerves juggle that, while your girl is in the seat next to you. Trust me, it doesn't make for a calm, cool ride. Grace had found a couple candy bars in the glove compartment, which had been sitting in there for God knows how long. At ninety what-not degrees, they melted into this ropy tar she didn't mind lapping off the wrapper. It found its way onto every part of her face except her mouth. Her hands left chocolate on the windows. She got caramel on the seat belt that still hasn't come out.

The rest stop was five miles away. We pulled into the third slot, down at the far end there. It was mid-afternoon, so this place was full of enough people to not see any particular person. I don't think I made eye contact with *one single person*.

My shorts had crawled up my waist, so the upholstery was clinging to my thighs. Grace is giggling at my hairy legs—these chunks of half-melted chocolate dangling from her teeth. She didn't understand what all the hours in the car had done to my patience, mistaking my irritation for some game. I wasn't talking, so she flipped on the radio, turning the volume up to some harsh static—only to smear chocolate on the dial.

That was it. My boiling point had hit. I told Grace to get out of the car. Slamming doors, deep sighs—the entire routine. Pointing to the curb, I told her to wait while I ran to the men's room.

I come back with a whole roll of toilet paper, finding Grace on the curb, crying. She's doing a better job at washing off her cheeks than I could've, the tears tasting more sweet than salty. We must have moped around for a few minutes, until she slaps a thick hand print of candy right across my cheek. I reach my tongue around to taste it, licking the bottom side of her palm clear off. I keep going back for more of her until there's none left. She's giggling again, so I start swiping the chocolate off her cheeks, too—until she's tickled back into having a fun time.

Good, I think.

A few sniffles later and she asked to wash up in the ladies' room.

She took the keys with her. Fetched them right out of my hand. They didn't fit in hers, poking out between her knuckles. It was as if her fingers had multiplied all of a sudden. I remember Grace walking down the sidewalk here—this stop-and-run between all the other families. She'd gallop along until someone walked in front of her, whinnying in place while they passed by, and then pick up her stride again once the path was clear. The farther she went, the more those keys sounded like spurs pushing her along. I watched her slip off into the crowd, and I remember wanting to keep looking at her. I'd stash the memory of this place in the trunk, with all our luggage. She would come back to me, and we would take that highway. Take it to wherever it led us.

I found more handprints wrapped around the seat. There were chocolate fingers pointing in all directions, navigating the toilet paper into deep crevices. Wherever I'd bury it, my hand would come up gooey, gummy. The candy wouldn't let go of the car, stretching out in long strands of caramel—only to lash back onto the upholstery. Even the sweets didn't want to let her go.

Five minutes passed and I fumbled for my watch. There was no sign of her. No smell of her. No taste anymore.

Women kept walking in and out from the bathroom, while I waited outside the door. That picture nailed to the front, that symbol or whatever you'd call it. She's a taunter, that's for sure. A stick figure in a skirt marking the ladies' room. She could have been a man wearing a dress for all I knew. But I'm watching her slip away and slide right back at me while all these women kept coming in or coming out. But none of them were *her*. I asked some lady if she'd see if Grace was still in there, but she came out shaking her head. There were dirty looks from everyone inside, but I had to walk in. I called out Grace's name at every stall. I kneeled down in hopes of finding her legs hanging in front of me. I just wanted to see familiar feet. Cream shorts down at her ankles. That's all.

No one had seen her at the vending machines. All the picnic tables had other families sitting at them. I'd spot a girl on her own and I'd think it was Grace. I'd run to her. The closer I got, the more the shorts wouldn't match, or her hair would turn a color off right in front of me. She wasn't waiting at the car. The phone booths were full of teenagers necking with each other. The walls had everyone else's name scrawled over them, but not Grace's. The parked cars kept switching with fresh ones. But I wouldn't let anyone drive off until I looked through their windows. Until I knew that she wasn't inside. I kept searching. Kept asking. Kept calling out, "Grace! Daddy wants to leave now!"

But that was months ago. Now I can't remember which finger of mine touched her last. What part of me she kissed before running off. All I see now are people on their way somewhere else, tangling up into each other long enough to relieve themselves. And then they leave. While I'm still here. You'd think people could remember seeing a face like hers. A head of hair as red as that, she could light her way through a crowd.

That's her, that's what she looks like. Sprinkle her with some freckles and she's good enough to eat. They're covering her cheeks, leaving her looking like a chocolate chip cookie. See that? She's smiling at the idea. This is the best photocopy of her, I think. All of these smudges could be sweet, if I rubbed them right. Because I'm sure she's still got a bit of candy on her face, somewhere. Think of the black parts of the picture as chocolate. And then you've got my girl.

You're coming through here at a pretty good time, now. This place emptied out about an hour or so ago. The weekend traffic thinned itself down to the serious drivers, like yourself. If you want soda, the vending machines are that way. I think I finished off most of the snacks yesterday, so I don't know how good your selection will be. The man who refills them doesn't come back until Thursday, so . . . sorry. My meals don't stray too far from potato chips and pop, but I'm not complaining. With the few handprints of Grace's still stuck on the car, you'd think I could scrape off a meal for myself. But I'd just end up smudging what's left of her over the upholstery. I want to keep her there for as long as I can. Let her fingers point me in the right direction.

I'm sure she thinks this is all some sort of game. That's what I get for starting our vacation off by feasting on the states. You can't help but choke once you forget to chew. And now I've got a bone in my throat that won't slip up the highway or down it.

I know she's still here. Caught right above the Adam's

apple, you could say. I've become so used to this place, even the people are looking alike now. I'm sure the same cars have driven through here two times over, at least. And I can't even find my keys. I've spent days looking for them, peering up underneath the stalls when no one's around. Getting real familiar with the plumbing. I feel like I have more in common with the drainage here than anything else. Their pipes are probably as clogged as mine are. Eating from these vending machines has left my insides feeling stiff. The fifty-cent foods here have become the staple in my diet, while the toilet feeds off of whatever I drop for it.

So there are a hundred and one different places she could be. Who's to say I've looked through them all? You have the woods, the toilets, the tourist info. All these cars.

Our car. It's been sitting there in the same parking spot for so long now, she has to know where it is. I've left a trail of candy wrappers for Grace, just in case. She couldn't miss it if she closed her eyes. It's been there for so long, it's starting to smell. I didn't think cars could rot, but ours is somehow. I haven't been able to get into the trunk, where all of our luggage is, so I'm thinking she might've brought along some pet and just not have told me.

It's these games. I can't keep up with them. I feel like I'm in the middle of one now, but I'll be damned if I'm not the last to know.

We're playing out a fairy tale here. I can't get to my shaving kit, so I've become some rest-area troll for her to hide from. I catch a glance of myself in the bathroom, or find my reflection in the rearview mirror. It's hard now to recognize what's staring back. It's hairy all over and just as scared as I am. It has an odor that follows me around, strongest in the places that I want to sleep. It's taken over the car with such a stink—letting me know that it's been there and will stay there for as long as it's parked in this place. And this is the part I have to play, while Grace is the princess running away, hiding from me. She has the keys, so she makes the rules. I can't leave until I find her. And I know she's close. God, sometimes I can almost smell her underneath all of this, she feels so close.

fox trot

A 79-year-old woman who fought off a rabid fox in April by holding on to the animal for 12 hours until help arrived has died.

—excerpt from *Richmond Times-Dispatch*, June 20, 1999

Only the good Lord knows what brought you here into my home, Mr. Fox. I keep no sheep under this roof. No geese for your stomach, I'm sorry. You crept in through the wrong door. You're not going to find anything inside this house but an eighty-year-old lady. And I'm afraid I can't offer you any-thing to eat—other than salted skin and mealy muscles. One look at my arms would be enough to lose your appetite, I'm sure. Not the most mouth-watering meal, am I? Once you tore through this gristle, all there'd be left for you to chew on is bone. And by now, they're brittle enough to crumble to pieces. What I couldn't fill with meat, I'd stuff with splinters. And to the throat, I'd go—lining every inch of your own swallow, shard upon shard.

That would be my revenge on you, sir. Eat me, and I'll devour you with a thousand more teeth. So tell those gums they better make room for me, Mr. Fox. For, if you're thinking of biting, your mouth will have to make way for a bite back. And my teeth will be just as sharp as yours, if not sharper.

Have my word on it, as an appetizer.

But my manners, dear. Where'd they run off to? They were probably frightened from your entrance. Sneaking your way through the front door like that, I'm surprised I didn't welcome you in with a heart attack. Here it's been two hours already and I haven't even introduced myself. My name is Mary. We'll make a good fairy tale together—don't you think? *The Old Woman and the Fox.* I like the sound of that. There's a ring to it, definitely. Fits my ears perfectly. Almost as snug as my hands around your neck. Where they'll stay, mind you. The moment I let go, I might as well consider myself bitten. My hands will keep to your neck like a collar for as long as it takes someone to save me, no matter how much your drool loosens up my grip. It's a sly trick, really. Pouring that poison through my fingers. As if I'd slip on your rabies. That's what I'm soaking in, isn't it? I can see it in your eyes, as clear as all of this spit. You are afflicted, young man. A sickness such as this leaves a fellow lonely, I'm sure. It takes over the senses, worse than love. To me, they were always one and the same. Working on a similar principle, at least.

Don't you agree, Mr. Fox?

You've caught a disease that heads directly for the heart, spreading through every vein it's tangled in. Before too long, there isn't a drop of blood that hasn't fallen under its spell. It must be hard to think straight, once it's taken hold. With the way it's left you drooling, I can only imagine what's stuck on your mind. Looking at me like that, you should be ashamed. I've already told you how old I am. I could tuck you into my wrinkles, I'm so withered. Pucker up to any pair of pleats that you pick. Lord knows I'm covered in them.

But I can understand how passionate you must have become since catching the ol' love bug. It's practically bursting out from your mouth. You're just waiting for the right lady to come around, aren't you? Cupid these days doesn't shoot with arrows, mind you. He's much smarter now. He gets diseases to do his dirty work.

But flashing those teeth doesn't impress me one bit. Claw at my arms all you want. Turn these wrists into red ribbons, if it pleases you—but I will not let go. Simply get that thought right out of your spoiled head.

Besides—this way, we have a little more time together. To talk. You forced your way into my house, so I think I deserve the courtesy of some companionship. You sit with me and get to know me before even considering getting near me with that dirty mouth. At least wait until my son arrives. Walter. He's due here tomorrow morning. That's what, then?

Only . . . ten more hours away. He's coming to take me grocery shopping. On Wednesdays, he's the alarm clock to my life. Always strikes the hour with his visit, making sure the house is all in order.

One morning not too long ago, he found me on the floor—my foot having fallen through. A pipe had sprung a leak somewhere in the basement. Sewage soaked through the floorboards here until they collapsed right under me. Swallowed my leg up to the thigh. I had been walking to the bathroom the night before, only to squat there until Walter came in the next morning. Had to do my business right there on the ground. It ran right down my leg, right onto the basement floor. The dripping kept me awake all night, as if my leg had become some stalactite in the basement.

Thank God it was Tuesday. If it had been Thursday, goodness. There's no telling whether or not I would have survived it. Walter would arrive the following week, only to find half of his mother hanging from the basement and the other half still straddling the upstairs bedroom.

He grew up here, he did. Birthed him myself, under this very roof. Memories like that soak their way into the wood, just as much as afterbirth has. And this floor has lapped up its fair share of me. Walter wouldn't know, but every step along this floor is upon family. That's comfortable for me, knowing that the people I love support me still. It's in the wood. What family never survived, I can find them here. Under my feet.

Look at what you're stirring up in me, Mr. Fox. Walter wouldn't approve, I'm sure. He finds it foolish of me to stay here, when the city is only an hour away. With all of its *Homes*. He is adding up the amount of repairs he's done on this house, warning me my time might be up here, if the ceiling springs another leak. Or if another wall caves in on itself.

But that corner, there? When Walter was eleven, he carved his initials into the wall with a nail—thinking I'd never find it. You think I would find a memory like that in one of these *Homes*, Mr. Fox? How much of this house would I hold on to, if I left it behind? I couldn't quite well take the door frame to the kitchen, could I? Where every inch that Walter's grown has been marked for years now.

My garden. There are more of my years planted into that soil than I could count. I'd say my sweat has fed as many of those vegetables as any drop of water has, if not more. Not to mention those pricks on the rose bush, pulling the blood right out of me. I feel as if I've begun to bury myself already, one drop of life at a time. I've even given the ground my children. Two. They came before and after Walter, one cracked egg at either side of him. What life they needed was soaked up into the floor.

Both of his brothers bring me strawberries now. If I couldn't tuck them into bed in my own house, I figured the next best blanket would be a strawberry bush. And now I pluck them at the end of every week, bring them back inside. Walter has only met them with his mouth. It's the only way I could tell him, really. All anyone has ever known of my other sons is through the sweetness they bring us.

I don't think I've ever mentioned it out loud.

See what you've brought up in me? See what you've got me talking on about now? Well, I hope you're happy with yourself, Mr. Fox. If I didn't know any better, I'd think Walter put you up to this—just to force me out of this house. But as I'm sure you know by now, sir, I'm going to keep as good of a grip on my life as I still can—no matter how much my arms are tiring. That was your little plan, wasn't it? The smell of this house must have your mind reeling. Is that what lured you this way? You're hungry for a vintage brand of blood. A timeless taste of generations, I'm sure. You want to lick up my life line, take what's left of my family. Is that how our fairy tale goes?

"Once upon a time, there was an old woman who lived all alone, surrounded by walls that had sapped her dry. Along came a lonely fox, starving for love to the point that his ribs raised through his own skin."

Is that how you want to begin our story? I never minded passion, Mr. Fox, but some things in life are sweetened with a little patience. Consider the fact that this is how they'll be writing our story, sir. Whatever you do from here on out, history will take it and turn it into a bedtime tale. This is a fable for the children, Mr. Fox. Please, take it seriously. You have generations of young girls listening to every breath, every move you muster. Let them hear about how much of a gentleman you can really be. I swear—the younger the man, the less time he has. I'd think you had never heard of romance. That's all a girl wants, now. And that comes with time. Good things come to those who wait.

Didn't anyone in your life ever teach you that? Should I?

Well, stop squirming. We're married now. The only ring we need is my hands around your neck. It bonds us together just perfectly. That way, we'll be holding on to each other forever now. In time, there will be just as much of you soaked into this floor as there is of me. From the looks of it, we're already off to a good start. Your mouth is a fountain for love. I feel as if you've filled in half of my wrinkles with your spit alone. I must look younger, already. Do I? I was very beautiful when I was younger. Keep pouring out the love and you'll see for yourself. Everyone will. Walter will find us here, holding each other. And that's how they'll picture us for eternity. In books, in all of the drawings— wrapped up in one another. Me cradling you, glistening in a wedding dress woven from your own foaming mouth. That's how you've proven your love. You're willing to water me with it. What Walter won't understand, the walls will tell him. The floor will know and explain. We've become a love story, Mr. Fox, for the children. For all the children.

the pool witch

Sizing up every slide Water World had to offer, it was as clear as chlorine to the seafaring three of Freddy, Chub, and me that our maiden voyage of the day had to be down the ride they called *Moby's Nozzle*. We, holding our post at the snack bar, could spot its peak halfway across the park, jutting out over the top of all the other tubes in homage to such spurts from the mighty whale's blowhole. Chub feared cramps as he finished the last of his hot dog, while the thought of discovering Davy Jones' locker at the pool's bottom sent a rash of goose bumps over my wet skin. Freddy, on the other hand, kept his cool. He saved his shivers for the pool witch.

"Who's that?" asked Chub, ketchuping his question with a final swallow.

And up Freddy's finger went, pointing to the tip of the Nozzle where she sat perched underneath an umbrella. The shade made it difficult for my eyes to make out anything but the red of her swimsuit. But it was a red to match the blood of all whose fate met that of the witch's, we three agreed. Not a nail on her fingers reached out for the sun, not an inch of her skin met the bright light that surrounded her. Shrouded in a cover of cool air, the only glimmer inside the shadow came from a silver-rimmed whistle she cradled on the tip of her lips. How that metal could catch a ray of light in the dark I never understood, but as Freddy was quick to explain, it was the very essence of her evil.

The lure was a simple one. Men of our age (which at that time was ten, eleven, and thirteen) couldn't help but hear from within our hearts the siren song of the fearful Nozzle, its height such a staggering one that many a bathing-suited soul wished to ride it. But before taking that lunge, one had to pass the pool witch. In her possession was the evil eye, cast upon all who crossed her path. So potent was her stare that when one rode through the Nozzle, the water would simmer up to a boil, reaching temperatures not meant for human skin. The only thing to land at the bottom would be an empty pair of skivvies, and the pool witch would have a fresh supply of melted flesh for tanning oil—the spirits of a thousand dead sailor-boys rubbed all over her body.

The trick for most was to scale the Nozzle and come down the other end—their hearts held tight in the grip of their ribs, their treasures still buried in the beaches of their Speedos. To finish such a feat and live to tell your mother about it on the ride back home was a sure challenge, there was no doubt about that in our minds. But Freddy had a whale of a plan, one to pale all others in comparison. Before Freddy was to ride Moby's Nozzle, he wanted to claim the slide for his own, with Chub and me as his first mates. But to stake out our territory on top of that chute, we needed to see the wench go down the drain first. If there ever was a treasure worth taking, Water World had built it. And if there ever was a foe worth defeating, it was the pool witch!

We had eaten our lunches before most swabbies even had a grumble in their stomachs, figuring we could have the run of the park while everyone else pillaged the snack bar. Our thinking was right, for there in front of us was a desolate slope: the Nozzle's lengthy tube coiling around a frame of steel girders—like a single vein still wrapped to a skeleton's wrist. At the bottom lay a pool so clean, it looked as if not a toe had been dipped into it. But we three knew what was really below the surface of that puddle of disinfected death. We knew that within its depths were the souls of children long since stolen looking up at us, praying for their salvation. I felt their weight on my sunburned shoulders with every step I took up to that hag. Even Chub had an extra pound on his conscience, giving the wood a creak with each foot he set down. Freddy, our fearless captain—he only scratched at his acne like the newly recruited teenager he had become—was a hero all right, and it made me proud to be amongst his crew. Halfway up the steps, he turned to Chub and me and said, "Beware the shine in her whistle. It's the heart of all that's black in a man. And beware the eyes. They've got devils swimming in them."

Oh, the eyes. I would have followed all of Freddy's orders if it hadn't been for those eyes! All it took was a glance from my own to see that hers were hazel—as green as the deep sea and as brown as the mud below it. I hadn't even gotten to the top of the steps yet before I was caught in the tide of her gaze. From her eyes I followed her hair—blonde by a bottle, but a beautiful blonde nonetheless—until I found her name-tag, pronouncing TABITHA in all caps, the letters sharper than a shark's bite. It was pinned to the strap of her bathing suit—redder than any blood I ever bled! It swallowed me up, just as if I had dived right into the spandex, bathing in the lives of those fated crewmen before me. She had me in her grips before I'd even seen the whole of her— her shaved legs as slick as eels, shaved as if a hair had never sprouted there before. It was a cunning disguise, *cunning!*, for the three of us knew under that sixteen-year-old skin, there was a witch to be damned . . .

"Are you guys going to ride, or are you just going to gawk at me all day?" Even her voice held a curse within it! Her words were the first strike against us, and they were filled with enough nettles to stun even poor Moby himself. Chub felt the blow the hardest, for, looking down at his already undersized swimming trunks, he discovered his sword unsheathing without him. Freddy's voice broke as he gave the cry to attack—*"Attack!"* And attack we three did— charging across the deck and pouncing on top of her. Chub took an arm as Freddy grabbed the other, oil-wrestling the hydra as best they could. It was a struggle to be sure, her tanning lotion greasing up Freddy and Chub's grip, causing their hands to slip.

Me, however—I found myself blinded by the reflection of her whistle, frozen in front of her and unable to lift a finger. But it wasn't the glare in that metal that hypnotized me, no. In the very throes of her body, I discovered it's really the sight of her tan-line that bewilders the wayward sailor, the pale hip where the swimsuit slips the true source of her powers. One sight of that ghostly skin and I was trapped in her port forever.

What could I do but watch on? If only Freddy and Chub knew that their struggle was nothing compared to mine, for I had to fight off the true horror of the pool witch. The shoulder blades she had were enough to slice through any rope—and how I wished they would cut through the straps of her suit. If there was only a way to get rid of that red and leave behind the white of her skin underneath, then, and only then, did I think I might have fate on my side. For it was her paleness that set my mind at ease, the lull of her foam-crested tan-line a song to my restless soul.

Somehow, Freddy and Chub had managed to reach the slide's mouth—just a few feet away from sending the pool witch down the Nozzle. Chub was crying, his face as red as her swimsuit. The front of his own trunks was wet, even though he hadn't been in the water for hours. Freddy could see it as well as I could: Chub's fingers were sliding down her arm, losing their grasp enough for the witch to shove her elbow in the pot of his belly. Chub dropped to the deck with his hot dogs spilling through the crevices—ketchup, relish, mustard, and mayonnaise all falling to the concrete below. Freddy hadn't a chance to see where he was stepping, waltzing into the puddle of Chub's lunch. There was nowhere Freddy could go but onto his back, slipping his way to his partner's side.

At that moment, the only two left on their feet were the pool witch, wheezing to the pitch of a whale-song ... and me. No other swabbie left standing but *me*.

I took in a deep breath, because I knew it would be the last I'd be taking. I closed my eyes, because I knew where I was heading I wouldn't want to see. My feet picked themselves up and leaped over both Freddy and Chub, and I found myself wrapped in the heaving bosom of the pool witch. Her fingers drove in my spine as she cried out in surprise. But I held on. Oh God, did my hands hold on! I snuggled my way into her swimsuit and prayed that the Lord would find me a safe passage to her heart—evil or not. For the pale of her skin sent me searching for treasures of love rather than land. Only desire could calm her raging waters, and I was brave enough to die sailing through them.

Together, we fell right back onto the Nozzle, our arms entangled in one another—setting our course straight down the shaft. She fought with all her might, her name-tag digging into my forehead—as if to whittle away my passionate thoughts. Her wet hair clung to my face like tentacles yanking my cheeks off. But we held onto each other the whole time—my head on her chest, the beat of her heart a sound I carried all the way down to the pool. And when we landed at the bottom, diving into the waters like an octopus holding itself together, then, and only then, did she ease up on her grip and cling to me like a land-lover to the sand. Freddy and Chub—they could claim the Nozzle all to their own, for I and the pool witch, a maiden to me if I ever saw one, sank to the lowest of depths in that pool, discovering a kingdom for our own and never returning to the surface.

the wheels on the bus go

The blessing of deafness would always unveil itself to me when Billy Dupres slipped his hand underneath my skirt. Empty ears were a privilege on the bus because, even though he would corner me in the backseat, spread me over the upholstery until I could read the book buried between my shoulder blades—I'd never have to hear his breathing. He'd drop it on me, let the exhale settle across my chest while the rest of him explored. The air in his lungs, wet as it was already, got me to sweat too, gluing my skin to the cushion. His hands and knees pinned to my every limb, he would stake me to the seat like I was his tent, something he could just slide into. But at least I didn't have to listen to his panting. It was easy enough to ignore his hands as long as I couldn't hear him moaning over me. *Feeling* him on me was one thing. But it's in hearing, I think, that people really dig their way into you. A simple whisper is enough to haunt you for years. Close your eyes, and the sound is still there, ringing through. But fate left me with an escape, something that would distance the two of us—a gap in my senses that he'd never be able to cross.

I'd never have to hear him.

He got picked up two stops before me. By the time I stepped onto the bus, he'd be waiting in the backseat. All I'd see was the crown of his head, his eyes book-ended by his ears—a pair of plastic snail-shells latched around the lobes. Billy was in denial about his deafness. He'd lost his hearing only a year ago. While cutting the grass, the lawnmower's gas tank exploded. The pop of metal never stopped in his ears, continuing to ring until it swallowed all the sound around him. When he came to, the first thing he saw was a plane coasting over his head. The shadow of its wings drifted across his outstretched arms, the two echoing each other. He said he'd never felt so close to a plane before. Where the sound of it went, though, he never knew. It's been hollow in his ears ever since.

But Billy was spared enough of his senses to use hearing aids. A satellite dish slipped into each ear, it looked like cement poured into a pothole—off-color and a little out of place with the rest of his body. Since there was still some-thing out there for him to hear, the other kids would make fun of him for it. We were a quiet bus, going to a quiet school. You were either all-deaf or not-deaf-at-all.

Bully for Billy. He was middling somewhere in be-tween the two. It's a hard decision to make when you have a choice, really. That's something I could feel for. I had re-membered sounds, felt a few whispers now and then from when I was younger. When my mother still had to wash me, two years old, I could hear. What I remember most is what water sounds like when it crackles against itself. It's a hard noise to let go of. My older sister—five years old—one day, she had the chance to play mommy with me. With the tub between us, my sister wanted to do right. Make Mom proud. She had done everything so perfectly, from putting a towel down at the tub's base so no water could puddle up on the floor, even to the brand of shampoo that leaves your hair smelling like oranges. She was looking to get rid of every germ I was holding, so she just let the hot water run, filling the tub up to the lip with a burning mouthful. She took me by the armpits, the tickles sneaking in with her fingers. There was laughter from both of us. Now there's a sound for you. Rises up and spreads. When my feet dipped into the tub, passing through a thousand degrees of teeth, my laughter changed its mind as soon as it felt the first bite. Up to my thighs in water, I couldn't understand the burn. There wasn't a feeling in me to recognize, anymore—nothing I could compare it to. It was a slippery sting, rolling over my belly as I tried to kick it away. But it kept splashing up against me.

Being two, all I had was a mouthful of words—and none of them seemed worth using. So I made new ones, brand-spanking new. I even threw in a couple sounds for extra measure, hoping my older sister would catch my drift. I used them all at once, running all my sentences on and on. Punctuation was just a waste of time, just to try to explain what was happening to my skin.

Before the sounds reached meaning, my legs gave out, the water sucking me into itself. When the rest of me went under, all noise just washed away. I remember the feeling of my ear drums melting under the surface. My hearing was bleeding away into the tub, like grime disintegrating off the skin, dissolving in the water. When my sister opened the drain, we'd find a ring of my senses strung around the porcelain.

If I wanted my hearing back, I'd have to scrape it off.

I'm still in the tub, swimming whether I am in the water or not. I have my head permanently under the surface. The pressure rubs against my ears, muffling everything. People talk, and all I get is this thickness of liquid, the sounds dragged into an undertow of garble. Words come my way through a body of water the size of an ocean. I'm hoping it drowns me sooner or later. All that's holding my breath is a faint trace of laughter. My older sister and me, the sound of us together. It's the only air I've had inside of myself for years now. It's been slipping out from my memory ever since, one bubble at a time.

That's why I didn't mind Billy's invitation to the back-seat. I'd wade through the aisle of the bus, passing all the

handmade jeers and put-downs. There was more sound inside of Billy's head than in any of ours, and I imagined it
had to be as wet as mine—the memories clinging to him
like pockets of air trapped to his skin. I almost understood
why he picked me. We knew each other, knew sounds these
other kids couldn't.

They just thought of him as payback. Who else was
there for them to pick on? They'd fling insults with their fingers, signing jokes Billy just couldn't catch. We all had ten
tongues to his one, his hands still mute to our language. Most
still considered him one of them, *The Talkers*—people who
took their tongues for granted, letting them wag like a tail
on an overexcited puppy.

But Billy wanted to show those kids. He wanted to
make sound through me, pitching his voice where a boy's
voice hadn't been before. Have it fill up the entire bus and
still go unnoticed by everyone. Something of a silent revenge. Even the bus driver wouldn't hear. She never listened
to us, anyways. Never had to. And the engine was too much
for me to match, even though I never heard it. I could only
imagine how hefty it had to be to drown me out.

Billy would wait for me, making it clear that he didn't
want anyone else to sit beside him. Once I'd step on the bus
and walk down the aisle, all the other children would keep to
their windows. The insult to them was that they all knew
what was happening, right under their own ears. The gasps,
the crying—they'd never hear it, even when it was only a
few seats away. It was as if all of their other senses could pick
up on the two of us—tasting the noises coming from us, feel-

ing it on the backs of their necks, while we defied the only
sense that really mattered. On the bus, we might as well
have screamed through the entire ride, all the way to school,
yelling over everyone's head until the kids could smell the
sound, see the sound. We'd even taste it on our tongues,
numbing the very lips we pushed our way through.

I stepped on the bus, found Billy in the backseat. He
was new to signing. His fingers stumbled over the words he
tried to conjure up, mangling his own thoughts. It didn't
matter, really. I understood him, making sense out of his
hands one way or another. No matter what he said, his fingers were always pointing to me, eager for me. And that's
what mattered. How could I turn a talk like that down?

"Hello." He groped.

I gave him a wave back, all five fingers.

"How are you?" Fumbling, dropping a couple words
along the way.

I took a heavy breath, the air wheezing in through my
throat. Breathing felt useless. There was sweat on me already, glossing up my neck as everything inside stiffened.

"I am scared." It read more like *I scare*, but I understood what he had meant to say. But it was my turn to talk,
my knees opening up to speak. Grabbing his hand, I
squeezed his fingers until they were all ears. I did my best to
sign *you can keep talking*, while forcing that hand of his underneath my skirt. The cotton lips sucked him up past his
elbow. I let him go, using my hands to say *talk to me, please*. I
wanted him to sign to me from the inside. I closed my eyes to
hear the words within me. This was where the two of us

talked best, where I could listen with all of my body and never miss a word. Billy may have started it all, but I was the one to keep the dialogue going. I don't even know if he liked it any more.

His two fingers sounded hot, a forked-tongue asking me if it hurt, if I was okay. I know I made a sound. I had to've. Something reached out of me, either to answer Billy or just to yell. But the air stirred, pushed by a force that lifted out from my mouth. I repeated everything Billy was saying—the words crawling up from inside one mouth and out the other. It filled up the entire bus, I'm sure. I know that. Like water loaded into the tub, we were drowning in so much noise. The surface raised over every kid's head and none of them ever even knew they were swimming in it. The only one who was listening was Billy. Which was beautiful. Someone was listening to me. Actually hearing what I had to say, no matter what part of my body it was coming out of. My breathing got heavy and it dropped on his shoulder. He told me so. He said it burned. I told him there was more heat where that came from, a whole tub full, and I opened my throat to its hilt, letting out all the boiling sound I had inside of me. Someone would have to crack open a window before too long, or they'd all fog over. Someone would have to balance out the hot with a little cold or we'd all burn for sure. Cup your ears or the drums will melt right out, like a blister popped from too much touching.

The bus driver had to wipe the window in order to see where she was going. With one hand on the wheel, the other brushed away the noise that had fogged up her field of vision. With twenty seats between her and me, we were on opposite sides of an ocean. No matter how loud I howled, she'd never hear what I was saying. All she caught was garble, grunting. Noises she'd never make sense of. But she turned around, anyways, finding everyone looking out the windows, oblivious to the backseat. Leaning over into the aisle, the wheel drifted with her. When she faced forward again, what she saw made her gasp. Not that any of us heard her. The left side of the bus was heading into the oncoming traffic. She jerked the wheel in the other direction, sending the tires into a stutter. The force of it separated Billy and me, our correspondence cut short, forcing us both back into silence. It felt cold again. All the sound I had vanished, leaving a distance between me and everything else. Billy was still holding his fingers in the air like a phone, alarmed at the abrupt disconnection in our lines.

We both looked up to discover all the other children turned around, gaping at us with dropped jaws. A hush hung in that void, the distance between their lips so empty, it was unbearable. With all of those mouths so wide open, with nothing coming out but whatever my imagination put in there, inside every last one—I believed I heard my sister's giggles reaching out from their throats, her laughter pushing past. It was all I could fit in their mouths, the only sound my memory had in stock. And it returned to me right then, spilling out from the hollows of a dozen children. *Quit your yapping*, I said, splashing their words back at them. *I don't want to hear what you have to say to me, anyways.*

spoonfed

The dinner bell rang the second the spoon hit the glass. You knew it was coming, didn't you? You're getting too smart for me.

Is Casey a hungry little sister today? Well, here's what I'll do. Since Mom and Dad aren't around, I'll treat you to a jar of applesauce. Cinnamon and all—no beating that. Now, I know we save applesauce for dinnertime. But since I have to feed you, I'll make it a special lunch. Sound tasty enough?

That's better than the meals Mom makes. She left out a bottle of creamed carrots for you—heaven and lips forbid. I know how tight your throat cinches at the popping of the lid. I'd have more luck prying you open a new mouth than forcing down a spoonful of that junk. Mom never understands, does she? I can always tell when she's fed you carrots. You'll be wearing them for the rest of the day.

But you're sixteen now. You're a big girl. The growing you've done goes unnoticed around this house, doesn't it? So this is what I'll do. When I feed you from now on, I'll let you pick out your own lunch. Whatever that tummy of yours is grumbling for, you can have it. How does that sound? If you want creamed carrots, then fine—creamed carrots it'll be. We can repaint the whole house with every bite you can't swallow, if you want to. But if you'd like some applesauce to loosen up the old plumbing, then just say it.

Name it and it's in your tummy, Sis. Right now, the kitchen's at your lips.

Knock, knock. Who're you going to let in?

What a good day it's going to be! Applesauce twice in a row, for lunch and dinner. If you can keep it a secret, your big ol' brother will even let you lick the jar. (And we know how much Mom doesn't like that.) Keep it between you and me, and every lunch from now on can be like this. Your tongue could be licking glass clean all day, as long as your mouth holds back from telling Mom. Remember what we call our secrets, Sis?

Hush-hushes, that's right. It'll be one of our own little hush-hushes, okay?

Now. Here comes the first bite. Down it goes—
smooooth sailing.

Like that? Smooth sailing. One swallow is all it takes to
wake up the rest of yourself, doesn't it? Like sunshine
spreading through your throat. I'd say, for a feeling like that,
it's worth a hush-hush or two. Secrets are only a sign of love
anyway, Casey. You know that? When you keep a secret for
someone, it's because you love that person enough to hide a
tiny piece of them—where no one else can see. That's what
makes a secret so special. No one else even knows it exists.
It's yours. It's a part of that person no one else can hold except you.

Second bite. Here it comes.

Moms and dads keep secrets. The biggest ones there
are, probably. They have to. That's the test in marriage, I bet.
It's all about whether or not a husband and wife can keep
each other's *deepest* secrets. And I'm talking about the things
you couldn't let your best friend know. Like the secret would
almost be untrue, if you never spoke a word of it.

If someone could do that for you, then it must be because that person's in love. That's what it takes.

Don't get so greedy, Casey. You're dribbling.

I'd keep a secret for you. Because I know you'd do the
same for me. I *know* you would. You're the best when it
comes to holding secrets. Like you were born for them. The
way your teeth curl in, that thick tongue—it's almost as if
Mom and Dad never wanted you to talk.

And I think I know why.

Casey! Hold still for me, okay? It's all over your chin.

Let the spoon do some of that licking for you. I swear—if it wasn't for me, you'd be lapping applesauce off the floor. If Mom and Dad came home and saw you on the ground, they'd never leave the two of us alone again. The whole jar is yours, don't worry. But take it easy. The slower you let the mouthful go down, the longer you'll have to enjoy it.

It comes in cold on the spoon, doesn't it? But once your lips seal over, something magic happens. It takes to your temperature. It matches your heat. The warmer the sauce is before it slips down, the easier it's going to be to follow it along, wherever it goes. And you'll want to keep with it, Sis. Because the secret of it all is: I think that's what love must taste like. If I could get my teeth around your heart, I'm sure I'd have applesauce squirting across my cheeks. That flavor right now? That feeling you've got running down your throat? That's me. That's my love for you. I've got so much to give, that I can jar it up and stack a whole shelf full.

So have another bite.

Do you want to hear a secret? You've got to keep quiet about it. If a word of this even comes close to the open, your teeth better hook it before it reaches your lips. All right? Nod for me, just so I'll know.

I'll get in closer for this one.

I know how to make love. Actually make it. It's as easy as apple pie. The sweet thing about it all is, you've got the seed for it inside you already. It's been there all along, in everyone—just waiting to grow out. Put a hand right where your ribs curl in, and you can just barely feel it knocking.

Knock, knock. Who're you going to let in?

The kick to it all is, half of those seeds will never see the other side of the soil. I'm talking about other people. Finding the right person. With everyone spread out all over the place, you'd think it would be easy to make a match. But life can become so tangled, if people let it. It gets easy enough to lose sight of those who're standing around the edges, you know?

You don't know.

Well, think of Mom and Dad. How blessed they were to find each other. They're the lucky ones. If I look at either of them hard enough, I can see one of them in the other. That's how strong their love has got to be—they copied each other. The shape of their faces is almost the same. I can swap Mom's nose for Dad's, and there wouldn't be a difference between them. You'd think they were custom-made to fit together. They're the lucky ones, Sis.

Then I think of when we were younger. I get to remembering the times when Mom put us into the tub together. I was, what? Ten years old? That made you seven? Balancing your body against mine was like looking into a fun-house mirror. I could pull off my clothes and be in the tub before Mom would've even yanked your shirt off. I'd sit there, watching her peel the pants off of you—finding the crust of whatever your diapers couldn't catch. And then you'd be naked, plopped into the water with me. It was hard for me to understand what had happened to you. I thought that in three years, you'd start straightening out, like me. Like everyone else. In my head, I'd try to go back to when I was seven—think if I could remember whether or not I

looked like that. I imagined everyone started off that way—
bent. That, in time, every kid evens out.

I was ten. Of course I'd think like that.

I remember Mom explaining the parts of you that
weren't the same as mine, using her finger to map out the
crooked spots. To try and flatten them with her touch. I'd get
embarrassed, because I couldn't make sense of it. Not because you were so different—not even the girlie parts—but
because it sounded like Mom was confessing over the nooks
that shouldn't bend that way. It could have been the water, I
thought—how it can wrinkle anything you dip into it. The
water was twisting you around. But the surface stopped at
both of our bellies, and you just kept changing the higher up
I looked. Not the girlie parts, but the people parts. And you'd
sit there, watching where Mom's finger went—following it
as much as I did. How did it feel to have her point at you like
that? Could you understand what she was saying?

I didn't know how to look at you. She took away any
understanding I had, and she never put anything back. No
explanation, no nothing. All she did was admit to your body,
with the way it was. Not by saying anything, but by the way
she touched you.

It hurt me. Mom was disowning you with her finger.
She'd cut any tie right off with the nail. And it changed the
way I looked at you. Not because you were sick with this or
born with that. But because I wanted to look. I wanted to see
what there was of me in you, and find the you in me.

I think I found it, Casey. It's not in any pictures here in
the house. I've looked. Believe me, there aren't many. It's as

if the run of our family starts with Mom and Dad and ends with you and me. I look for a photo that reaches out past us, and there's nothing. Not a one. The two of them are so wrapped up in one another that they've cut off everybody else—taking the pretty parts of each other and fixing them together. It's uncanny to see how much love can blur the lines between two people. How there is a power that can marry the good and squeeze out the bad. If Mom and Dad could do that, Sis, what would happen to all the ugly parts?

Look at how pale we've gotten. All those fingers Mom gave you, they were lessons for me. They weren't there to help me understand what had happened. Mom never wanted that. All she ever intended was for me to know where your mouth was, where the diapers went. That way, I could take care of you—and the two of them could leave. They've tucked us into a shadow, Sis. Look at it any way you like. We've been inside this house, keeping their secrets for years. These curtains never get opened and the shelves are always stacked with enough creamed carrots and canned peaches to last us until we both rot.

Whatever their secret was, Sis, we came along because of it. They probably have another house they go to, with real children—where they spend the day in the sun, *chewing* their lunches—while we sip and swallow smooth bites that never take any effort. Because you can't, Casey. You don't have the right parts to do it. You've never been showed enough love to grow beyond baby food. And it's left you all twisted around.

So what has it done to me? I look at my reflection in

you, and I wonder where I'm growing wrong. The only place I can think of is inside. Because when it's the two of us in the tub, everything within me starts to tighten. The second I get into that water, my heart wants to take root in you, Sis. I want to make up for lost love. I want to feed you. Think of Mom and Dad, Sis. They were so perfect for one another because they'd been plucked from the same tree, already. We've got love bred in the bone. It's instinct. It's natural.

Here. Take a bite, but don't swallow it. Take it, Casey. Let the sauce settle over your tongue. Let it ooze underneath.

Feel how sweet that is? There'll never be a drop that makes it off your chin, will there? Your tongue is too quick for that. Your mouth never had such a good friend. Between your teeth right now, you're tasting the closest thing to heaven. Your mouth is a treasure chest.

You want to finish off the jar? Then let me help. What? You think you could actually get your fingers around the lid? Or would you try to find another way inside? How about licking through, until the glass wears down and you've rubbed out a hole for the sauce to bleed. That's love for you. It's got the conviction to flourish in the most muddled places. It always finds a way to grow around whatever chokes it. No matter how knotted your limbs are, Sis, your heart would find a way to get in. But a hug right now would have applesauce squirting out from your ears, wouldn't it? It would get in your hair. Your pretty brown hair. I've got to be more careful. Too much of this stuff could drown you. The key to caring is to feed the seed just enough that it grows up nice and tall, reaching out for the next bite—while not to soak the poor thing, so that it gags. We want to keep the spoon coming, nice and smoothly. No dribbles here, Sis. You'll swallow it all. The hush-hush is—I've got no one else to give the love to.

So let's dig in.

Talk about a toothache, Howard. There's this pain in my molar that won't stop throbbing. Woke up with it in my jaw, over there on the left. Hey, no surprise. Found my mouth flung wide open again, third time in a row. My chin was on my chest, yawning all night. Easy enough for some termite to crawl right down my cake-hole, make his way through my throat until he finds himself a soft spot. I'm not wanting to worry over every itch I get now, Howard, wondering whether or not I'm being chewed on from the inside out. It's on my mind all the time, nowadays, that I'd say I've got a couple woodworms squirming through my skull. I'm feeling them finger around, that's for sure. The pudgy little grubs keep brushing up against my noggin, fumbling around in there like a bunch of thumbs. And now they're plumbing into my mouth like it's their own friggin' flower garden. Some termite's going to pull up a bouquet, tugging on my teeth like this. It'll leave me lisping, before too long. I'll be gumming up my words from here on out, if you don't take better care of me.

I'm coughing up sawdust already, Howard. (*Eh-eh-eh.*) See? This cavity's just a taste of what's coming, trust me. What good am I going to be after I start falling apart on you?

Who will talk to you then?

That *wife*?

Didn't think your right hand knew what the left was up to—did you, Howard? You thought I wouldn't notice that extra notch next to your knuckle, but I felt it rub over my ribs the second you slipped into me, reaching right up for my mouth. The pain pinched onto my molar and still hasn't let go. Wrapped so tight around the roots, I'm practically tongue-tied over it.

And guess what flavor I found. Something sour. Something a little bit on the bitter side of my taste buds. Wasn't rubbing my tongue over a termite, I'll tell you that. But metal. *Metal*, Howard. In my mouth. The second I licked it, that tang rusted over my palette, taking over every other taste. Until I couldn't spit it out, even if I tried.

You got yourself a wedding ring, Howard. And you didn't even tell me, your best friend. Wanted to keep your secret under tight wraps, so you thrust your fist up where I couldn't find it. Making me the ring-bearer by hiding it up my ass. But hello, what's this tickling my tonsils? Thought I woke up with a gold tooth, fixing onto that halo. But no, that's a wedding band back there, flickering through. My mouth has got to make way for your marriage vows, now— swallow them all whole. And all I get in return is the aftertaste. Now how fair is that?

My lips can't make sense of it, Howard. My voice sounds different, I'm so stiff in the throat from it all. It doesn't feel like I'm even talking to you, anymore. Somebody else is filling the words in. I'm the one with the ball-and-chain cinched onto my chops, weighing my jaw down so that I can't even shut it when I want to. It just hangs there, dangling to the ground a little more each morning. Stretches out my cheeks so much, they're starting to flap around. You're chumming it up with a butter-churn, I'm sounding so sputtery now. It's embarrassing.

Why are you doing this to me, Howard? Your hand is shaking so much, I've got shivers running up my spine. Don't be such a tight-lipped, limp-wristed sissy. You knew you couldn't keep me in the closet forever. I'd find out, whether you told me or not. I'm not your plaything, you know that. We share something. A connection. There's more of you in me than you're ever going to find inside of that w-*wife*.

Ah, I can't even say the word without choking on it. A *wife*, Howard. Who are you trying to fool, here? I'm not some

dummy, now. Better not treat me like I am. Don't think you
can pull one over on me, just because I'm pulled on over you.
I can tell how long it's been since you last slipped in by how
stale the air is inside my mouth. If it's been a while, I'll
know just by breathing. When it's stagnant between the
cheeks, when my lips are chapped enough to shed splinters,
well, it's pretty easy for me to see you've had your hands on
somebody else. I can even feel it on your fingers when you
dig in. You're a little softer in the skin, like you've been
wearing another glove. Might as well come up to me with
lipstick smudged across your collar, for crying out loud.

    And you still expect me to talk to you. Simply sit on
your knee and act as if I don't know a thing. You bring your
ring-finger into me, let it wriggle around my mouth like a
termite, *some queen with a gold crown*—and I'm supposed to
just let her chew me through? She's come in between us, you
know that. Starts with the ring, oh sure. You're wearing your
better half like she's some little finger puppet on the side.
Sticking your digit through the hoop must've been hard,
Howard. Takes better aim to shoot up such a tight hole. But
once she swallowed past that first knuckle, Howie, she sunk
her teeth in. And is she ever going to tear you to pieces. She'll
never let you go. Won't let up, even to breathe. I should
know—she's starting in by nibbling on me! Getting rid of
her competition by eating me out. I got a whole head full of
termites, now, from your pinkie to your thumb. It's a regular
hive up here. Your fingers are tunneling through my whole
body, giving me more veins than my heart can handle.
Spreading my love so thin, I'm nothing more than skin. I'll

be a husk for you to hold on to by tomorrow. A glove and that's about it.

Do you hear what I'm saying? Am I talking to myself? You'll never be your own man, Howard, ever again. Peel me off and you're all alone. Nothing but the bones stripped down. People were puppets once, too, you know. They just tightened up their asses enough to save themselves from being fucked over all the time.

So where's your spine, then? I know where mine is. And I'm going to use it for a change. I've got no backbone until I'm sitting over your forearm, fine. But whose fault is that? You've always been so impotent in the wrist, you left me with a speech impediment. You're a pansy, Howard, no matter where you hide your hands. But once you slip them into me, they're mine. Your fist swells up into my head until I can think for myself. Thoughts burst through my brain that I never had before. And I can share them. Your fingers make muscles for my mouth to move with. And I speak my mind. I wake up to you, Howard, opening my eyes to your face every day. And it fills me. There's not an inch of my body that you can't call your own. My lips are yours. So use them. Please, it gets so hollow hearing myself mouth off like this. Throw your voice around all you want, you're not going to find anybody else who can listen like me. What's this *wife* going to give you but an ear to whisper into, maybe a shoulder to cry on. Me, I throw my whole body into it.

Oh come on, Howard. All I'm asking for is what's between your wrist and elbow. That's all. I'm empty without you. You've forced your way into me so much, pried past my ass enough times, that when you're not there, I sink into my-self like some hollow shell. All you ever leave me with inside is a wave goodbye—and then you just drag your hand back, stealing everything you give me to begin with. I'm the old layer shed over and over, leaving behind your fresh fingers like larva just hatched. Baring that soft hand for everybody else to see, while I just rot off into sawdust.

Well, I don't want to let go of you. My ribs will grip on to your arm, if they have to.

Once you find a hole to hide inside your *wife*, you're going to realize how much of you is still hanging out in the open. Too shallow for your tastes, I'm sure. Can't reach her throat, can't squeeze out sounds from her esophagus like you could with me. The best you'll get from her voice-box will be a moan. A grunt and that's all. You'll never get your voice into her, Howie. Her body is just one big dental dam. You two won't fit together, take my word on it. Nobody goes this deep. Not like me. Hey, forget about your ring-finger. That's amateur, if you ask me. I'm swallowing you up to your elbow, Howard.

And I never spit.

michelle

These woods are bringing back memories. Could have
been just yesterday we were trudging through here, looking
for Michelle. I had volunteered for the search party, being
her next-door neighbor. A friend of the family's and all. First
in line, if I recall. Got the honor of leading the group out,
twenty men total. Walked alongside Michelle's father the
whole time. I could see the hope flicker across his face, coming and going like the sunlight blocked out by passing under

these tree branches. Bill turned to me once, about an hour into the woods. Looking me in the eye, he said, "She's angry at me over not letting her stay out with her friends. Got herself this new boyfriend she won't bring home, so I went and gave her a curfew. I know she's been sneaking out, anyways. But Hayden—" He stopped walking, gripping my arm so I'd fall back from the front line. "Hayden, she's always come back home. She's never been gone for this long. Her mother's getting real worried and I don't know where to look for her anymore."

We're going to want to take a left, now.

We combed these woods with the kind of care I remember Michelle taking with her own hair. You couldn't have found a crooked tree after we raked through. Just long, narrow paths stretching out from their backyard. That's where we started. The twenty of us partnered up, counting off right next to their swimming pool. It'd been a gift for Michelle. Sweet sixteen, I think. Her father and me had dug up the hole while she was at summer camp, surprising her with a new pool when she came home. There wasn't a day when I couldn't look out my window and find her back there, swimming July away. August away. The whole summer. She'd climb out with her curls clinging to her shoulders, that sandy blonde turning a deep brown. Funny that I'd think it, but—when she disappeared, it'd been raining on and off for a couple days, matting down the leaves into a wet brown just the same. And here we were, stepping over them, the leaves sticking to our boots as if we had just marched over Michelle's hair.

We've got to walk down this way for a while.

She didn't have a new boyfriend. Michelle could've cared less about the boys at school. That's something her father never understood. Bill wanted control over who she dated, worried to death that those troublemakers at school would snitch her virginity. He would throw these pool parties for the whole neighborhood, hoping one of the Brighton twins from down the street would come along and ask Michelle out. Tim Brighton had just scored a perfect 1600 on his SAT's, while Jim had been elected captain of the high school baseball team. Bill practically tossed Michelle out to them. Either one, if not both. Should've seen him at these parties—dragging Michelle over to Tim. Or Jim. Whichever one was closest.

Nothing ever happened. Just as well. I mean, her heart was in that pool. You couldn't find it in anything else. In anyone.

In the morning, I'd wake up to water crackling between her legs. Didn't need to set my alarm. Her breaststroke woke me. I'd come to the window with my cup of coffee and there she'd be, toweling off to get ready for school. Brushing her hair.

"Morning, Mr. Peters," she'd say, smiling, a bit of hair slipping into her mouth. "When are you going to come swimming with me?"

Couldn't give it much thought, really. I mean, I tried. I tried not to think about it. But she would say it to me just about every morning. Teasing me by flicking her towel at my window. A drop of water would strike the glass, dribble down

in front of my face. And I'd flinch, thinking it'd hit me.
That'd get Michelle laughing, every time. *Bull's-eye.*

Hold on. I think we walked out too far.

I'm sorry, we've got to double-back some. I'm starting
to see the highway through the trees now. You hear the traffic? Yeah, it's coming just over the bend, there. You can reach
it from Michelle's backyard in thirty minutes. Run it in fifteen, no problem. It would have been easy enough for her
to've just crossed through the woods, step out onto the highway. Flag down some guy driving past and that'd be it. She
could've been in someone's car before her parents even knew
she was missing. Cross the state line before Bill would even
think about checking back here. And she would've done it,
too. She could have. Mentioned it to me every chance she
got. Until I had to listen to her. Believe her when she said it.

I mean, Michelle said a lot of things to me. Things I'd
have to brush off before they could settle in. When she'd
catch me at my window, the invitation was on her face before I could turn away. Just this bend in her neck, motioning
towards the pool. My breath would fog up the glass enough
for her to disappear, diving right into the water. I could be in
any room in my house, and I'd still hear her kicking, her
legs chopping through the pool like leaves crumbling under
my feet.

She'll be wearing her swimsuit. This baby-blue one-
piece. There was a shine to it, especially at night. When the
people driving by have their high-beams on, the light
stretches into the woods a bit from the highway. I was just a
few steps behind her, when all of a sudden, her swimsuit
caught some of those headlights; this flash of blue before

going back to black. Another car would pass, and I'd see the blue outline of Michelle streaking through these woods. She was shimmering from being so wet, running in between the trees like a silverfish slipping through my fingers. I could see the leaves clumping on around her bare legs, just below the knees; hear that crackle under her feet.

Her parents had been at a Neighborhood Watch meeting, leaving Michelle at home alone. I'd been in the kitchen, finishing up my meal when I heard the pool part its waters, letting Michelle ease right into itself. I got the faucet on to wash the dishes, letting one rush of water drown out the other. Because this had been building up all summer. I would wake up at my window rather than in bed, staring out into my next-door neighbor's backyard. Seeing the stillness to the pool before Michelle went swimming was sleep for me. I couldn't wake up until she dove in. Got under my skin. Only way I could fight her off was by turning the volume up on the TV. Or hide in the farthest room possible. Or purchase a pair of headphones. I wanted to be strong about this, I swear. But when every kick from her leg sends a shiver through that pool, you can't even imagine what it was doing to my spine. Nearly had my back broken by the time I finally walked over. And she didn't realize I was standing there. Kept swimming back and forth, her body gliding through the water with the ease of breathing. I mean, *she was on the air I inhaled.* She might as well have swam her laps through my lungs. When I'd breathe in, she'd swim to me. When I'd exhale, away she went. Back and forth, like that. Back and forth.

The smell of chlorine was so thick in her skin, it stripped

away any scent the dogs could've used to find her by. It was strong enough to taste, even. This pure flavor burned over my tongue, like kissing lime. Michelle had soaked up enough chlorine to cleanse away any foulness I felt for feeling like this. I couldn't even tell you what it felt like to touch her. There was nothing to taste, to smell that she could've called her own. The pool had peeled it all away. What was left was this wisp of a girl. Nothing more than the skin. That made it hard for me to hold myself back. All I followed through these woods were the sound of leaves, the fresh smell of chlorine, and the flash of a blue swimsuit holding this spotless body.

It was better for Bill to think she ran away with some boyfriend. I began believing it myself. Their pool hasn't been touched for years now. Michelle used it, no one else. Now the only thing to dip into the water are the autumn leaves, falling from the trees and collecting over the surface. They'll float there for a while, sinking under once the water soaks through. Swallows them all whole, forming into this sludge at the bottom.

And I can't help but think of Michelle. Found myself at the window a few days back, and I thought it was her, her brown hair, floating just below the surface. That smell of chlorine slipped away a long time ago. What I'm left with is rotten wood. Years of it. She's been out here long enough for most people to forget. But every time I hear the crackle of dry leaves, I think Michelle's swimming back to me.

When she finally realized I was standing at the edge of the pool, her breaststroke dwindled down to this doggy-paddle, treading water where I couldn't reach.

"Can I help you, Mr. Peters?" Her mouth had been just at the surface, one lip below, the other above, and I could see the water creep in.

Told her I was ready to take her up on her offer. Go for a dip. She grinned, the water brushing against her teeth, saying, "You can't be serious, Mr. Peters. You're friends with my father."

I was. That's why I led him right past her, making sure he didn't notice the upturned dirt. Bill doesn't look into these woods to find her. He sees the highway and believes she's still on it, hitchhiking her way into oblivion. He doesn't even notice these trees. This little patch of ground, here. What's under the dirt has been for me to reason with and nobody else.

Walking back that night, I realized I was covered in so much mud. Had to take a dip to cleanse myself. The pool was warm, the water rinsing off any imperfection, erasing every scrape down to the skin. I drank from it, lowering the surface down an inch at least; taking in so much chlorine that it burned to breathe. Washing Michelle all away.

second helping

Wieners roasting over an open fire. Now there's a smell I could follow for miles.

Think I did, sir. Ma'am. Sorry to spoil your family's camp, stumbling in like this. But I couldn't help myself. Hang your hot dogs over a flame like that and they'll start sweating off their lard. You hear that fizzle when the fat first drips into the fire, slapping over-top a hot cinder and sizzling back into the air—*snap, crackle, pop* all around. It's perfume for meat-eaters like myself. When I first caught wind of that aroma, Oscar Mayer over the pyre, it took hold of my nose like a leash.

Led me right to you.

Billy Higgins. First year Bear Scout, troop number 245. Can't quite tell you how far I traveled, but I'm sure my toes will testify to a thorough journey. Which ones are left, at least. Pretty safe to say my stomach's wearing more of my shoes than my feet are. Ate the laces off years ago. Wrapped tongues with my Nikes, too. Just to tide me over, see? I knew I'd find help sooner or later, if I just held off on anything above my ankles.

And then came that first hint of fat. Heard that hiss of hot-dog grease sprinkling against your kindling. Only rain I've ever known to smell like meat.

Mind if I? Can I eat? Just one, *please?*

My troop and me set foot into these woods ages ago. How many years, I'm not so sure anymore. Hard to keep track after I counted past all ten fingers. Tougher even, after eating my pinkies. By the looks of my uniform, I'd say I've been out here for a *real* long time. When we first walked into this state park, I had to roll up my pants so I wouldn't trip over them. Now they're starting to creep up over my knees. These bracelets used to be sleeves, I swear. I've popped off almost every button since. The hair on my chest sprouted out in a thick crop. Pried past these threads, until they rooted into my uniform. Couldn't take my shirt off after it became a hairy prairie, even if I wanted to. Half of my Bear Scout badges have dread-locked into my chest.

And I was hoping to earn my camping badge out here. We all were, all ten of us. Me, Freddy Stern, Marvin Mumford, Max Moore, Zack Knighton, Adam Forest, Robb Sandagata, Michael Hearst, Joshua Camp, Brian Lennon . . . The whole neighborhood. Mr. Mumford, our scout leader—he was newer to the troop than any of us were. The man wasn't even certified to head our group. He'd stumbled into the job after our real scout leader, Mr. Stern, came down with the flu. He was Marvin's father, the only boy in the lot to earn his over-a-hundred-pounds badge. Mr. Mumford would bulldoze through the brush up front, his armpits leaking enough butter to soak up into his khakis—all those rolls of fat looking like a stack of pancakes. Marvin would be heaving away in the rear, a good ten yards behind the rest of us.

We were book-ended by butterballs. Marvin's belly pressed so far up against his shirt, you could see the buttons straining. His shirt was untucked, fanning behind him like a turkey tail—in *obvious* disregard to Bear Scout regulation number 63. In the handbook, it states that, *"While in public, on duty, or in the midst of one's fellow Bear Scouts, no cub shall present himself in any form of disarray—including attitude, well-being, or apparel."*

And Mr. Mumford hadn't even noticed. The rest of the troop knew it, sensed it from the first step into this state park. Mr. Mumford wasn't a true Bear Scout.

Freddy was the only one in the group who knew how to make a fire, so he had the honors. We had our hot dogs dangling over the flames in no time, the limbs of processed pork plumping up at the ends of our sticks. They swelled from the rise in temperature, waking up with the warmth. Watching them ripen from all the heat was to witness the miracle of meat blossoming into full bloom. You could smell it budding in the air, a meat potpourri. Even when they started to char, we left them in—searing the pink off their skin until they'd been branded in ash. All ten of us were looped around that bonfire so tightly, our wieners crowned the flames—our grace rattling through these trees.

> *Living the life of a Bear Scout,*
> *is the only life for me,*
> *Where glory, honor, and duty,*
> *are my holy trinity.*

> *I thank my fellow Bear Scouts,*
> *for the food in front of me,*
> *I'll never go on hungry,*
> *in my new-found family.*

We sang so loudly that the song still echoes through. I hear them when the wind is low enough. The leaves will rustle up like goose bumps, even after all these years. Nothing but a grumble in an empty stomach, really. You'll hear it, too. Sounds so slight at first, you won't believe your ears. But give the song some time and it'll creep right into your camp. Clings onto your senses, for sure, no matter how deep you dig into your sleeping bag.

They're out there, you know? In the woods. Can't tell you how many, but . . . safe to say there's at least five. Maybe more. Hard to keep track after all these years. Some of us couldn't take the loneliness at first, getting so tired of being tucked into a sleeping bag. When all we wanted was to go home, see our mothers again. Only lullaby we had out here was the Bear Scout hymn. I'd hear it in the middle of the night, after everybody had fallen asleep. Marvin would whimper it into his bag—the top cinched off, sealing himself inside. Thinking nobody was listening. But I'd hear him sing, finding myself quietly following along. Until the words were watering in my mouth. Watching Marvin's breath brush up against his sleeping bag made him look like a talking hot dog.

None of this would've ever happened if Mr. Stern had led out the troop. We would've earned all our badges that weekend, every last one. Instead, we were forced into eating what few badges we already had—pretending like they were Girl Scout cookies. The *real* chewy kind. After that first month, Mr. Mumford couldn't find a way out of this park anymore than his own feet. Every grumble within our stomach must've burned up a pound in him. You should've seen the man sweat. It was slipping out of every pore.

One night, I woke up to find Mr. Mumford sneaking the last rations of raw hot dogs! The rest of the troop snapped out of their sleep to see the meat still bulging in his cheeks, a limp digit dangling from his lips . . .

And none of us said a word. Mutiny made its way to our mouths by other means.

These sleeping bags make for great Hot Pockets. Mr. Mumford's mission was simply to supply the meat, after we hung him from a tree branch. He dangled over the fire Freddy had lit, the sound of his sobs bloating up in his bag. I worried he might drown in there from all those tears. He salted himself up pretty good inside. That sleeping bag burst open in a piñata of pork, our meal diving into the fire. We ate so deep, his ribs combed back our hair.

This was the true initiation into the Bear Scouts. We were nothing but a block full of cubs back at home—but we didn't want to be boys, anymore. Waking up that morning was to forget about our lives beyond these trees. Home for us was now a nylon pouch, warm enough to be our mother's womb. We kept to the flames, the light casting our shadows across the woods behind us. Our black figures projected onto their trunks, possessing these trees. The spirits of our Bear Scout forefathers surrounded us in a ring of flickering hands and feet. Their souls encased by the bark, their branches would bend along with our dancing bodies. All ten of us looped around the fire, gripping onto that hot heart so tightly, our wieners crowned the blaze. We didn't want to be *men* like Mr. Mumford. Who wants to grow up with role models like him? We wanted to be Bear Scouts forever! So by dipping our hot dogs into the flames, we seared off what was only weighing us down. And if we cried, it was because we found out where to bare the bravest badge of all. Right between our thighs. The smell of burning flesh lifted into the air as our spears brought up mouthful after mouthful, the ethereal lard roosting in our lungs—giving us the breath to break out into song.

> *Living the life of a Bear Scout,*
> *is the only life for me,*

Where glory, honor, and duty,
are my holy trinity.

I thank my fellow Bear Scouts,
for the food in front of me,
I'll never go on hungry,
in my new-found family.

Bad place for your family's camp. You're resting on sacred ground. Weren't the empty sleeping bags hanging from the branches enough of a warning for you? We let these trees collect our crusts. We simply suck the cicadas right out of their shell, leaving the rind behind. Only way you can make this easy on yourself is to slip back into those sleeping bags, cinch yourself in tight.

'Cause tonight, I get the feeling I'll be earning my buffet badge.

and the mothers stepped over their sons

Well. A skinned knee would be a blessing now, wouldn't it? You'd all thank God for a bullet in your thigh, rather than that one embedded in your head. If only those soldiers aimed their rifles a little lower. Now how's that for a thought to have rattling through your skull? Better than the buck-shot, I'm sure.

You boys play too hard.

Look at all of you now. This field is littered with so many fresh faces, it's like sifting through fruit that's already fallen from the tree. The war waited until it could pluck you up from your mothers' arms, let a bullet or two chew through your ripe skin. And once the guns got their fill, well, they simply tossed you off into the grass. Just left you to fester into the ground. Let the worms eat the rest.

Yesterday, the air couldn't keep itself quiet. The rifle fire spread for miles, reaching all the way home to your mothers. It echoed for hours, pecking at your parents' ears. We had no choice but to listen, all of us. We all had to hear the gunshots rattle on until it sounded more like crows overhead. And we all knew, boys. When the air finally went silent, we all knew what had happened here.

Now none of you will ever see the other side of nineteen. Here you are, back to nap time before noon. This field is a nursery for young soldiers. With your arms up stiff in the air, you look as if you're all reaching out for your mothers. I've never seen so many empty hands, clenched onto nothing but rigor mortis. It'll be dark before any of you lift your heads off the earth. And when you do, it'll be by someone else's hand, probably family, flipping you over to lay claim to what's left. Nothing but your bullet-ridden bodies.

So don't hide from your mothers, now. Turn your faces over so we can see. We're only searching for our sons. You'd tell me if you were laying next to mine, wouldn't you? My child had red hair before the bullets even cracked open his cranium.

Michael? No point in hiding from me. Pouting like this only keeps you from your coffin. I'm not leaving this field without you, and that's a promise. You come home, let me

bury you where you belong. I don't care if I have to drag you
back by the boots, young man. And believe me, I'll do it.
Most of us mothers will have no choice.

Yours will want to scrub those cuts up before burying
you, little boy. Wipe those wounds until she can see your face
again. It's unfair to hide under all that dried blood. For her,
I'm sure, it's no different to've rubbed your cheeks free from
any food you covered yourself in as a child. We pride ourselves in licking our fingers and polishing those cheeks. Let
them shine like apple skin. Don't want to confuse your dim-
ples for those bullet holes, now. Do we?

Michael? Your friend here has as many freckles as
you do.

Oh, sorry. Freckles keep to your cheeks. They don't rub
off that easily. I can't help but think all this blood is a part of
your face . . .

Michael? Michael?

There are so many of you to choose from. It'll be days
before you're all sorted through. But your mothers will flock
to this field soon enough, don't worry. We're the vultures
now, pecking away at every corpse until we find the one
we're looking for. Even after that, though, there's bound to
be a few of you left behind. The crows will be your parents,
then. They'll have to take care of you. Consider your body
bound to the ground by worms, otherwise. They'll rope you
down and won't let go. Rooting you to this field forever, if
you're not careful.

Michael would know better than that. He was a smart
boy. More brains inside his head than that helmet could

hold. He was going to be a teacher, you know that? He would have taught your children how to handle their arithmetic if you hadn't have handed him a firearm. You see, when you boys were out hitting each other with sticks and stones, he kept to his home. To his family. A child like Michael deserved to stay inside, where he'd be safe. His lungs were too delicate to overuse. God gave him nothing more than tissue paper to breathe with. One cough could tear his chest into tatters, if he wasn't careful. And I told him that, time and time again. Roughhousing just wasn't something that his body was built for. He needed soft walls to protect him, paper thin. So I put him behind a book. Every time he wanted to play outside, I barricaded him within the walls of a novel, where air is as light on the lungs as ink is on the page.

You have to understand. He couldn't even wear his uniform without his shoulders slumping over. He'd never had that much weight on his body before. His canteen strap nearly choked him.

But Mom, he pleaded with me, *Mom, let me go.*

He was nineteen years old. The war had already fed on his father. Now it wanted a second helping of my son. My little boy was wearing a uniform that had been fitted for a man, his own sleeves swallowing up his hands. His collar hung so low I could see the stem of his neck, his head just waiting for some soldier to come along and uproot it like a radish.

But he wanted to play with the rest of you. It wasn't enough that you boys bullied him every time he walked home from school. You had to let him enlist. Have him march to the beat of his own hissing breath. His lungs could have sounded the infantry, he must have been wheezing so loud.

Michael! Look at your friends now. They're all so ashamed for what they've done to you, that they can't even look at me. They have to bury their faces in the mud so I won't recognize them. Well, when I see your mothers, I'll tell them all what you did to my boy. How you dragged him out here when you should have known better. He was weaker than the rest of you, you knew that. His body was meant for fertilizing minds. Not this field. And now all he'll ever amount to is a mound of dirt in some cemetery. That's all any of you will ever be. Do you hear me? I should hope you're all left here in this field forever, until the grass grows over your bones. Until everyone forgets you. You should pray your family can remember what pair of underpants you left the house in, because it'll be a miracle if there's enough of your face left to identify once the crows sweep through. With these uniforms and your half-eaten fresh faces, you all look like you're coming from the same family. Well, I feel for the mother who has to step into this field, find all of her children like this. Nothing but a bunch of mud-soaked soldiers who forgot to come home for dinner. Who made their mothers walk for miles just to drag them back. Bury them next to their fathers. Leaving the rest of us behind. Your mothers are all going to be buried alive in their own home. These empty houses lining up next to each other will be tombstones to dead families.

You think I'd let Michael leave me like that? Have him walk off with the rest of you, his lungs trumpeting the cavalry call? Only for me to haul him home by the boots, his legs in my hands, the rest of his body plowing through the field while I towed him? Doesn't a boy like Michael deserve to stay at home?

You boys might as well be Michael. All of you. With blood sprinkled over your cheeks, you look like you're wearing his freckles. With your head open wide, your hair is as red as his. You all look like Michael. Like my boy.

When I heard the rifles tear the air open wide, I could have sworn it sounded just like his lungs in the midst of one of his fits. He was having one when he walked out the door, his body weighed down so much, his face was blue. He was yelling. Spitting up lung at me when he said he was leaving whether I'd let him or not. Firing off coughs. Choking on his own breath.

And then it went so quiet. The air just congealed over.

I've been looking for hours over the same bodies, watching them stiffen more and more each time I pass by. I think I've seen you a hundred times over, but then the color of your hair rubs off on my fingers. Turns out only to be blood. Michael. If I keep calling out like this, your friends are all going to want to come home with me, begging like little pups for me to pick them up. Take them back with you. I don't think I'm strong enough to drag them all. I can't do it.

You'll just have to wait for your own mothers. None of us were strong enough to hold on to you boys. Hide you at home until the war blew over. What are your mothers going to hold on to now? Where will they all be without their sons? I'll tell you. Here. In this field. With their very hands, they'll rake through until they pull up on the right pair of pants. Reap their own babies. Someone's going to have to stay by, in the meanwhile. Keep the crows away until the mothers flock through.

Michael always knew. Mothers make the best scarecrows. They keep everyone away from their sons. They keep their children at home.

Leave these boys alone! Any piece you've pecked off of these children better make its way back to their faces or I'll pluck every feather from your body, one at a time. Until you're the ones covering this field. Until your limbs freeze over, those bare wings pointing to the air, like broken fingers reaching up for your home. Where you'll never be able to go back. No matter how hard you try.

Put that back! You stay away!

As if these boys didn't have enough holes in them already.

honey well hung

Got my breath spread out before me like mayonnaise, it's so damn cold. I could rub it over one of your wings and have myself a sandwich. Take a dozen of your fowl-fruit here and make me some egg salad.

Any of you hens would like that?

Nothing out here but us chickens, my ass. Someone's sneaking into my coop, plucking up my poultry. Had my mind set on shooting me a fox a couple weeks ago, I was sure of it. Started off simple enough. A chicken missing every morning. Nothing left but a couple cracked eggs, the yolk all soaked up into the ground.

But no fox has it in himself to do what's been done here. A fox has got teeth, I know. But teeth can't lift a chicken eight feet off the ground, noose the poor thing from the roof, hangman-style. And just let it dangle there until it's shitting out however many eggs it's still holding. I walk in here every morning only to find another spine snapped, one more bird slung dead in the air—its wings all outspread. You chickens better tell me what I'm dealing with here. It'd all be in your best interests to fill me in, 'cause there aren't that many left of you. If I got to spend the night numbing my hide to find out, then consider it frozen to the floor until that cock crows. But don't think I'm happy sitting out here, when I got a house only a few yards away.

It's an empty house now. You know that. Got no one else to live in it but me. Two wives in the ground, no children to speak of. Nothing left but us chickens, right?

My ass.

Now I got someone trying to take you all away. My own livelihood. I've been peddling poultry for years, and this is the thanks I get. Inherit my father's farm once he flew the coop. Built myself a shed, and there I go. I'm raising chickens by the mother lode. I'm making ends meet by setting myself up a stand down on the highway, selling eggs to drivers-by. Get all kinds on that road. Vacationers, businessmen. Everybody's looking to bring home a fresh dozen, squeezed out from the hen's behind by the very hands that're selling 'em.

That's love. Now you're the only family I got left.

There had been some promise in this being a family

farm. Long time ago. Had myself a wife just starving for a baby. Eleanor. She'd open her legs to me like a newborn bird snapping at the worm, if you know what I mean. We were both hungering for it, together. Get ourselves some children to fill up these fields. Let 'em run around with the chickens. Ellie had herself some blue eyes, letting me know we had a boy on the way. I'd wake up to them every morning, staring me down. She'd have this grin in her, telling me I wasn't getting out of bed until I laid down some chick-feed for that little chick-seed.

Couldn't tell you how many times I pecked away at her, hoping to crack into that yolk. Every evening before heading to bed, Ellie'd rest her wrists right where her rib cage opened wide, letting her fingers stretch over her tummy—until the tips touched just over her navel. She'd know the baby'd be coming when they couldn't connect no more. That's what she kept telling me. She'd lay in bed, rubbing down that flat belly. Just waiting for something to crop on out. Before she'd slip off to sleep, she'd whisper to me, "My angel's gonna lift my belly up to heaven."

For months, I sat on that highway, my crotch feeling as squeezed as fresh Florida orange juice. People'd turn off the road and pick out their dozen. In what little small talk there was, I'd get around to telling them about Ellie. How we were holding out for that belly of hers to bulge. I told so many customers about her, I bet you half the people who passed through that highway knew about my wife without even meeting her once.

Wonder if they ever think about how she's doing now.

Every time I came home from the highway, I'd return

to Ellie's belly, same shape it was before. As flat as that field. Not a bump to speak of.

So we'd have at it again. Couple of little lovebirds.

Finally started to take a toll on her. At night, I'd catch a glimpse of her stomach, finding these scratches all over it. Ellie was plowing through for real now. She was searching hard for that baby, thinking I might've misplanted my seed.

Now you tell me how to handle something like that. I'd try talking to her, and I might as well've been speaking to myself. Every day that baby didn't decide to lift up on her tummy, until she started thinking it had something to do with her insides. When Ellie'd fall asleep, I'd lift up on her nightgown and see that she'd plowed down into her own self. I could follow those scratches all the way into her undergarments.

Now you tell me how to talk to her about something like that. Only thing I figured I could do was get her that baby. And get it in her quick. 'Cause from the looks of her legs, she'd been digging deep.

I'd wake up and Ellie'd already be out of bed. Gone off somewhere. I'd find her here, in the chicken coop. She'd be kneeling down in the hay, rummaging around.

And all of you were squatting there, watching over her like she was one of yours.

The day I come home and found her hanging from the roof here, I felt a drop within my pants. Before my heart even had a chance to break, my damn testicles fell. So quickly, they clacked against each other in a loss of hope or a sigh of relief.

You pick.

There was no stool knocked over, no chair under her

feet. Ellie must have gotten the rope over a high beam, then slipped that noose on like a necklace. And with some strength, some hearty determination, she had to've taken the loose end of that rope and pulled her own self off the ground, one heavy yank at a time. Without letting her own chokes get in the way, she had to hold herself in the air long enough to tie up the very rope that was strangling her.

And all of you just sat there, staring, following her dance. As if she'd hypnotized you with her swaying. Her body waving in the air, goodbye.

Now, Ezra hadn't been a neighbor exactly.

But she lived close enough to know where along the highway she could get her eggs. When she heard about Ellie she was just about as shocked as one could be. Drove right up to the stand. Not three seconds out of her Pontiac and she's letting out some heavy sighs, dropping a lot of tears. Her face found my shoulder and she just started bawling. Wasn't until she looked me in the eye that I realized Ezra wore makeup. Funny for a woman who lives all by herself, I thought.

Asked myself, now who is she trying to please?

At first, I couldn't tell just who she was fixing all of these self-proclaimed "heavenly scented" omelets for. But in the few months following Ellie's death, I'd say Ezra bought up to about half of my stock. Becoming my most prized customer. Purchased half a year's worth of eggs before I even asked her to marry me.

When we were moving her boudoir from her old home

to mine, I took a break in her backyard to catch my breath. Only thing I caught back there was a horrible stink, a smell you only find downwind of the devil's ass. Discovered her compost pile, overflowing with five to six hundred eggs. She must've been dumping a dozen every week, letting 'em crack and bleed over one another. Crack and bleed.

I couldn't help but stand there, thinking to myself.

So much motherhood just up and gone to waste.

Ezra's legs whined for a kid and I just couldn't shut 'em up. Felt as if something was going wrong in me. Something that would wake me up in the middle of the night, some voice whispering out from Ezra's thighs. It was soft, sweet-like, inviting me to give this woman the gift of a baby. But it sounded like Ellie, like she was calling from in there. As if her ghost was doing some ventriloquist routine with Ezra's legs. Had to do something about it. You tell me what you would have done. Me, I answered the call. As best I could. It was the only thing to get Ellie to quiet. You hear me? Only way I could muffle her was to fill up her mouth.

But Ezra didn't spit back no baby.

No nothing.

She swore to me that she was built for breeding, hips and all. But damn it all if I couldn't get the seed in her. I'd say Ellie had possessed Ezra's poon-tang, spitting out what I was trying to slip in. But she'd keep pleading with me to give her that baby. And I'd try. I worked so hard at it. Ezra would drift away and it'd just be me pecking at an emptiness. My sex out of breath, wheezing my seed, my testicles were a pair of airless lungs about to collapse.

After months and months of hopeless humping, that empty feeling went from my balls on up to my heart, this void sucking what little spirit I had left. Ezra was still thinking about babies, for Christ's sake—while all I had on my mind was her damn compost pile. All of that life rotting away. When she'd ask for a little lovemaking, I'd bury myself into her, thinking I was fucking that pile. There'd be no babies in there, no sir. Not with me at the helm. Just shell and dribble and empty creation.

To spite her, I'd force Ezra to collect the eggs in the morning. She'd return with her hands all covered in red speckles. I took pride in you chickens for pecking at her. Every time she'd reach out for your babies, you'd give her your beaks instead. Just like good mothers should. Like any mother would.

So. When Ezra hadn't come back from the coop, I'd figured she'd just given up on me. I thought she'd left. I took my time getting out of bed. Walking to the shed, I assumed all I'd find was an empty basket.

Not Ezra hanging from the roof here, dancing in that familiar step.

I could hear the beam warp under her weight. This tiny shed, so small, echoed in her last spasm. Until it went deep into the ground, the sound snuffed out by the earth. And my God, if I wasn't the slowest dimwit this farm had ever seen. Understanding slapped me hard. Even with Ezra rocking back and forth in front of my face, I couldn't seem to focus. All my attention went to my testicles.

Ellie, sweet thing.

And you all just sat there. Each and every one of you, squatting on top of your own children, protecting them from me. Kept staring me down, acting like I was the one you had to worry about. But that's not so. Ellie's the one getting envious with you here, not me. With all of this life spitting out around her, what do you expect? She's keeping this place an empty farm. For everyone. You hear?

I'm paying for this problem I got in my pants. What's hung in there is as good as dead. Just like everything else on this farm.

But what else is there out here but us chickens?

Right Ellie?

My ass.

Let's liquor up and have ourselves a pumpkin pie show!

Lick her? We hardly even know her.

Hey, hey. That don't matter. 'Cause we're dealing with *vegetable* matter. We prey on pumpkins, boys. They never mind. What's a farmboy to do on a Friday night, but amble out to the field? There's an acre out there claiming to be the closest thing to heaven, this side of the sky. Holy ground for loins the likes of yours and mine. I'm talking about the pumpkin patch, boys. A stretch of land like you've never set foot on. In the summer, that field is as flat as a five-year-old girl. But come fall, puberty strikes Mother Nature and up pop her pumpkins. With a little patience, that ground is going to give way to God's gift for you and me—dozens of them. They cover this field, ripe enough to the touch to feel like skin. Human skin, if you believe me. Close your eyes when you grip one, and you might as well be holding somebody in your arms.

And they won't complain. Won't say when enough's enough.

Carve yourself a hole, and you've found yourself a haven for harmless humping. It's a heaven, by God, and nobody gets hurt. It's just you and Mother Nature, wrapped up in one another—until your seed mixes in with the pumpkin's.

So who's with me tonight? We sure as hell aren't getting any younger. And those pumpkins will be gone once winter hits.

Win her? We hardly even know her.

True, true. But what are you looking to do? Court the damn thing? It's a melon, for Christ's sake. What goes on under a full moon is a farmboy's business, and no one else's.

Take me. I've lived out here my whole life, all eighteen years of it. My parents held me at a field's length away from everybody. I tell you, there ain't anything that stunts a boy's growth more than a farm. Look out my window, and what do I see? Soil. And miles of it. Corn covers it up in the summer, and pumpkins in the fall. They reach well on into the horizon. The world might as well be covered in crops to my eyes, from my front yard on around the globe to my back porch.

Call me the Christopher Columbus of corn, why don't you?

The only time I ever asked my father where babies come from, he pointed to the pumpkin patch. I was still soft in the skull by his standards. He must've figured that'd be all the birds and bees I needed. Taking me by the hand, we crossed through the cornfields that fenced in our house. He had me pull off a cob, shuck it free of any foreskin. We came to a clearing within the field, the ground overtaken by vines. Here it was: my father's pumpkin patch. Felt like I found his hidden *Playboy* stash. Dozens of them rested along the ground, their roots all tangled amongst each other—like a slumber party of girls, asleep on the floor, their hair weaving into a mesh of blonde, brown, and green.

"See, son—it goes a little something like this. Boys got these and girls got this. Boys get it in their mind to go where the girls ain't so acquainted with yet. It ain't exactly clear that either/or are going to make sense out of each other's parts, asides from pissing with them. But by taking this . . ." My father waving the cob. ". . . and planting it here . . ." My father driving the cob into the pumpkin. ". . . a little magic takes place."

He kept sawing the cob through the shell, the squish of the pumpkin's insides filling the air. When he pulled out, the cob shined in an orange glow. It glistened under the sun like no ear of corn I'd ever seen. There was a polish that tempted my fingers to touch its kernels. I asked my father if I could have it. I kept that cob until I knew I was alone, whereupon I ate it raw. I licked that wetness away. And was there ever a sweeter ear of corn?

No sir. Never on my tongue. Honeyed to the touch, my lips were savoring her flavor for hours. I'd finally tasted the heavenly nectar!

Neck her? We hardly even know her.

What's a little romance to you? The moon was full! It gave my breath a blue glow. I was panting so much that the air surrounding me was as thick as fog. Even though it could've been twenty below, I was working up such a sweat. I could feel the lower half of my spine lashing around, like a whip cracking against someone's thigh. And oh my, the feeling I unleashed into that pumpkin . . . I'd say, the howl that pulled up from my throat was loud enough to deafen every ear of corn in that field. Let those stalks go limp with my moans!

Hey, boys. It's true. This world is covered with them. I have yet to find a corner of this country that doesn't have a crop. And you know what stays the same, no matter where I end up? Farmboys the likes of you and me. Now, as alone as you're feeling, believe me—you're not. Far from it. When you're hungry and got no one to turn to, then look to that field. Just as corn nourishes the belly, pumpkins appease your pants. So harvest yourself some honeys, boys! Pleasure's waiting, only an acre away . . .

Ache her? We hardly even know her.

The feeling will grow on you, believe me.

the man corn
triptych

part I: man corn

I'm striking this match and leaving the rest in your hands, Lord. Can't rightly untie myself from the stove now, can I? Not with these knots, no. Not after what I've done. Hog-tying myself to the furnace is a just punishment, in my recipe book. I'm fueling this fire with every impure thought I've had ever since winter hit, and I'm hoping it's enough to burn the house down with me. Nothing here deserves to stand tomorrow morning. Let the crows peck at the scraps and ashes, for all I care.

Not that there'll be much left for them.

Katherine blacked out not too long ago. I took it as my sign to finally end all this, before either of us succumbed to another hunger. 'Cause we got it, Lord. The both of us. It's taken root in our stomachs and neither of us can yank it free. If you think I'm not ashamed of what's happened under my own roof, then let this fire prove it. I'm just praying that you might mention to Mother Nature tonight to cover up our leftovers with a little bit of her snow—so that tomorrow morning, you won't look down on your good earth and see the blemish we leave behind.

You just got to understand, Lord. Winter took a bite out of my family's fodder from the very first frost. Living as deep in the region as we do, what we eat comes from what we grow. And we're a family that's accustomed its palate to corn. Our summers are spent pulling up ear after ear, until the crops are left deafened for another year. By September, our basement is usually full of enough food to last us through the bitter months—a belly so stocked on corn it aches from every corner.

But this summer sure wasn't one for the picking. We had hoped for an early rain, knowing another drought like last year's would wither away any shot at a good crop, for sure. My wife, Molly, got on her knees as early as March, praying for it to shower. We even asked Katherine to solicit your services for a little favor from Mother Nature.

Remember us calling, Lord?

You wouldn't let us forget. When you dropped your rain and wouldn't let up on it, the summer storms sticking around well beyond their welcome, my wife had to hunker back down and beg you to relent on the weather. The heavier your showers, the thinner our soil, watering the ground down until our cornstalks couldn't grip the dirt anymore. Their roots slipped up from the mud, like fingers losing hold of the earth. I sat at my kitchen window, right here, watching them all tip over one at a time, right on top of each other; our succor slumping over into the mire. Corn-dominoes.

My family sat at this window all summer. We witnessed our chances at survival this winter drown. What corn we could salvage was too soggy to sink our teeth into.

Bloated to the bone. Soaked in the cob.

You gave our food to the worms, Lord, letting them dig into our meal as if the corn itself was a corpse buried shallow. Our field became a graveyard. I'd lift up on a stalk like I was dredging the dead—its corn-silk hair all muddy, clinging to its own ears. A sponge to your rain. The notion of eating never turned my stomach more. Here we were, Lord: a family of three, with nothing to shuck between us. Molly had always followed the Bible like a recipe book to proper living. Never left out a single ingredient. Which made this tough for her to stomach, I'm sorry to say—a pit forming inside there all through the fall. We had nothing, Lord. Save for prayer.

Now how could we eat that?

The sounds of worship swept through our halls like a smell lingering from the kitchen. I'd get my teeth around a blessing or two, hoping to keep my hunger at a distance. Chew on Jesus for a change. Every meal was marked by grace. Not much more. But Molly insisted. Even without anything to be thankful for, she wished to fill the air up with prayer. If we talked about you, we could put our minds on something other than our stomachs. Fattened ourselves up on you, we did. I thought I was going to retch once the winter winds wrapped around the house, tasting the same damn prayer, day after day. I almost heaved from so much talk. Had to use my mouth for something, sure. But my tongue was tiring of your words, Lord. I wanted to fill these cheeks up with something I could really chew.

I even caught myself sleep-walking one night. I don't know for how long or just where exactly I'd been, but I woke up with my hand on the doorknob to Katherine's room. Had it cracked open enough to peek inside. There she was, sandwiched between her sheets. Looking all sweet. She was mumbling numbers in her sleep. Counting sheep, I imagine.

Catching them, eating them. Not sharing a bit. I woke her up by slamming the door.

When winter hit, I'd watch the wind try lifting the stalks up from the field. Since the mud had frozen over, most of the cobs just jutted out from the ground. Looked to me like the field was hungry itself, row after row of yellowed teeth—just waiting to eat. Winter was going to have its way with us by frostbite, I was sure. I couldn't keep the cold from working into my own mouth. That's when you know you're going to freeze. Your teeth tell you so. Something about that wind heads directly for your lips, sinking into your gums, digging down deep. Won't take too long until they wrap around the roots, the chill tries to pull itself up a meal. Good God, you feel the cold grip on.

Who's become the food now?

Molly was finally realizing how hopeless her divine diet really was. I think it struck one day, when she allowed Katherine to play in the snow outside. If it got her out of the house, along with her bellyaching, Molly saw no problem with it. Katherine was always complaining, *Mommy, feed me this.* Or, *Mommy, feed me that.* So Molly saw no problem in her playing outside at all. She looks out the window and finds Katherine making a row of snow-angels. Of course, she got a bit proud, watching her daughter surround our house with prayer. Then she watches Katherine walk back to her first angel, kneeling down at its side. Only to start eating at it. She took that first angel's head and spread it into a gnawed patch of snow. Angel number two had its wings chewed away in no time. Three lost its feet. By the end of the afternoon, they were nothing more than a row of white blemishes wrapped in teeth marks.

She put Katherine to bed early that night, wanting to talk with me about *what we should do.* As she's talking to me, her breath comes spreading out of her mouth in a pale puff. The house had grown so cold that we could see each other's exhales now.

I could've sworn I smelled corn on her breath.

You tell me how it got there, Lord. I wouldn't know. But you could be sure that I was reeling from it. I leaned into her, taking in deep whiffs. I swear, I would've been in knots all night if I hadn't shucked her free from her clothes. All I'd hoped to do was lift up some corn, if you know what I mean. There are other ways of getting your mind off of hunger than prayer. Off the cold. Why did it always have to be by blessing you? I mean, you can understand that—can't you Lord? There was love in her mouth, I smelled it.

What was under her clothes, though. Ribs raised high. My wife's stomach sunk low. Such impure thoughts can come along with skin. I kissed her, square on the belly button. Katherine had come from that oven years ago. I just wanted to check and see if there wasn't anything left on the rack.

Molly was shivering so much, I couldn't tell if it was from the cold or from me. Something in the way that she stared at me, I don't know. Like I held her heart in my teeth, showing it off to her. All I could think to do was kiss her again.

The wind reached me before I could get to the door. Molly had run out of the house before I could even explain that all I'd been after was a little love. She ran right into the snow, cutting through the cornfield. Once the doorknob was in my hands, all I could see was white. White, everywhere; the snow coming down hard, swallowing Molly into the drift.

What to tell Katherine? That was my night for you, Lord. How could I explain this to my daughter? After stewing away the early hours of the morning, I must've just given up and passed out. And dreams came to me. More than had ever come before. I woke up to Katherine jumping around me, my hand in hers. "Corn, Daddy!" she yelled, the liveliest she'd been all winter. "We got corn!"

She yanked me up from the floor and dragged me over to the kitchen window, pointing to the field. It took me a while to wake up, wiping the potatoes from my eyes. Only to focus on our barren crop, so pearly white I would've thought we were looking at your teeth. Only a few bites away from getting swallowed by God. That'd be the day.

But prodding up from the snow was a single stalk pointing straight into the air. A bit off-color from the corn I was used to, but hell. Beggars aren't choosers in this house. I got bundled up and took to the field, with Katherine running right behind me. Starvation followed, as if it were a new member of our family. And sure enough, me, Katherine, and her new brother, Hunger, all stood around that meager little cornstalk, just barely budging out from the ground. It reached an arm's length off the ground, a slight bend in the elbow, with five finger-sized cobs curled up at the top. It was something of a miracle, I'd say. Together, Katherine and I pulled up on the stalk. It was a struggle, for sure. Each budge tugged up more, uprooting a hefty trunk. For such a small shoot, it sure did have a lot of growth under that snow. A half-mangled snow-angel rested where we yanked the corn up. Funny how nature does that, I thought.

The way my wife knew she'd made a satisfying meal, she always told me, was by how quiet we all were when we ate. If we kept to our food and left out the talking, then that proved it. Well, dinner had never been more silent. Now our kitchen's littered in oddly curved cobs, all of them pecked clean.

But here's my fear, Lord. It's Katherine. She's been getting some hunger pains that I just can't keep up with. She blacked out a while ago, so I thought I'd take the opportunity to check. You know, see what she's hiding in her tummy. I crept into her room so I wouldn't wake her. But in lifting her shirt, I wasn't prepared to find all that corn. I mean, rows of it. Stalks lining her chest, caging in her heart. She has a crop raising up from her flesh already.

And it left me hungry, Lord. Such impure thoughts can come along with skin.

Why else grant us the pleasure to taste? When it's so heavenly to butter up these ears with a little drool, sprinkle salt onto freshly shucked flesh. One touch of the tongue is all it takes to yearn for the flavor for the rest of your life. And I am hungry for it, Lord. I have never starved so hard in my life. The temptation lies in the aftertaste. And ever since I've eaten from it once, it's gotten a grip on my mouth, taking me by the tongue and pulling me in. Just for another bite. One more.

So if you don't let this match make a meal out of me, then by God, I beg you: Don't look down on this house for the rest of the day. Don't ever look down on me again, Lord. Because I'll have myself a feast only a fire could let you forget. Let it devour everything under this roof before I'm free from these ropes, Lord. You better let me burn while I got my hands tied in prayer. Otherwise, the only grace you're going to get from me will be in silence. Where you'll know just how good the meal you made in your likeness really is.

part II: gretel wendigo

You're weighing me down, Daddy. I need a rest.

All these trees are making me dizzy. I'd say they were

reaching for me, if I thought I had anything to offer them. But what have I got now, other than you? I have my fill of family, and that's not something anybody is able to take away.

Momma had told me a bedtime story once, where this brother and sister were out in the woods, playing well into nightfall. After a while, all that daylight was soaked up into the trees, slurped up over their heads by the leaves, *schlup, schlup*. It went black before they even thought about saving some light for themselves. Running in the dark got them more lost than we are now, Daddy. We're lucky that way, I guess. We still know where home is. I can see a glow coming from over the hill. Almost looks like the trees are on fire, but I know that's just my eyes playing games.

They do that a lot now.

Won't be too much longer before there's nothing more for the flames to eat. We'll be left in the cold once the house burns down.

When I first felt it, Daddy—the fire, I thought I was waking up to heaven. There was a warmth on the other side of my eyelids, a gust of heat brushing up against my face. When I opened my eyes, I was hoping for angels. Wings and all, with a pair to spare for me. But when I saw the walls on fire instead, my bed full of flames, I knew I was still at home. The heat was reaching for me before I could even wipe my eyes. Then I saw that I didn't even have a blanket covering me, anymore. All I was wrapped in was sweat, my shirt on its way to ashes.

I was breathing through my nose the whole time, smelling myself cook. Now, how long had it been since I'd smelled meat?

That's when the story got into my head. About that brother and sister. It just popped up. *Ding*, like a dinner bell. I was in the same bed Momma had told it to me. She'd said that the two of them had been lost in the woods for some time, hoping for a way home. Then one of them gets this smell in their nose, warm and sweet. They start following it, letting it lure them through the woods, like they'd closed their eyes to let their noses lead the way.

I can understand that. Winter freezes everything over, until it all smells empty. What's there to sniff out here that's fresh? Winter creeps in and takes it all away, acting like a spoiled child. He never shares. I'd be lucky to make friends with a snow-angel. I'll plant a few into the ground, wrapping this whole house in a ring of cherubs. But the next day, the snow takes them all away.

I want to know who this winter doesn't like. Make them my friend.

He's nabbed our house, Daddy. Look at the snow covering it up. It's as if our home was never even there. No wonder you set it on fire.

You'd never let winter touch me. You'd rather have the flames swallow me whole, than ever let this snow lay a hand on me. When I woke up, I raised my ribs high above my skin, ready for them to grab onto that fire and hold it tight. Here's a friend that the snow won't go near. Here's someone who will stick with me. It'd protect me against that chill. You think I minded a little burn? Not when friends are this hard to come by. I stayed in bed, letting the story Momma told me take over. The fire tucked me in this time.

That brother and sister followed the smell through the woods. Being left alone wasn't such a scary thing, anymore. That's what I needed to hear. Something to say that the cooking was okay. I had a flavor of fat frying in the pan. Now when was the last time I'd smelled that? I got to feeling so greasy, the scent was sizzling up from me. My belly was so empty, I filled up on the aroma. I fattened up on air alone.

And it made me hungry, Daddy.

You can understand that, can't you? I ran straight to the kitchen, and there you were, hugging the stove with flames all around. You were cupping the fire. And it got me greedier than Gretel, Daddy. Momma knew what tale to tuck me in with. 'Cause when that sister saw her brother roasting in the stove, she discovered a hunger that she could never share. Not with anyone. Sure, she had it in her mind to save her brother. Sure, that's what she was thinking. But no one has ever mentioned what was going on inside her own stomach, have they? Has anyone?

Well, it was easy to read in between the lines of that grill. I understood. She had it in her stomach to save her brother, too. To get him out of that house and keep him all to herself. When I pulled you off the stove, you burned my hands. The roof of my mouth still stings.

The front door crumbled right as we passed through. Another second in the house, and we'd be ashes about now. My feet feel like they're burning, but I know that's just the snow. The cold has already leapt on our home, now that the fire has died down. There won't even be a mark on the ground before too long. It'll be blank by morning.

My belly is so heavy right now, I don't think I could run anymore. Just thinking about standing up makes my stomach turn. I got to hold onto you. Can't get sick. Otherwise, I'll have to lap you back up from the snow. And I'm not doing the cold any favors by sharing.

I wish you could see the fire, Daddy. What's left of it leaves the snow looking yellow. Everything's got a glow to it, like corn. You should take a look at me. Butter me up and I'd be good enough to eat.

part III: wendigo relic

I'm good for a little gangrene, if we don't get my leg to a doctor soon. I don't need to look at the wound to know where that smell is coming from. Just a wipe of my eyes to clear away this sleep, and it's simple to see that everything below the left knee is worse off than yesterday. This only happened two days ago, and already the punctures have opened up to an infection. My leg did a cruddy job of putting on its decay, that's for sure. Those punctures are lined with too much green to look pretty. There's enough soreness surrounding them to leave my leg looking like it painted on too much blush. Now no one is going to want to touch it, no matter how colorful that rot dolls itself up.

I stepped into my own death, now—didn't I? We're the ones hunting through these woods, and I'm clumsy enough to walk into someone else's snare. It felt like a bear-trap, at first. But worse. Stepping through that skeleton's chest, the bones closed right around my leg. Those ribs clenched on tight to my shin as its spine snapped under my boot. It had been so mechanical, so precise, as if this was what skeletons were meant for.

I fell over right away, fearing my leg would tear off right then and there if I kept walking. My rifle tumbled a few feet to my side, leaving me at the whim of whatever was eating me. That's when I realized that it wasn't steel chewing into me. But bone, rather. Four ribs, two on each side, each one sinking into my calf. I let out a yell when they first sliced through, watching the bones sponge up in red. They were porous enough to leave room for a little bloodletting, soaking up plenty of me. You'd think that skeleton wanted to live again with the way it was suckling. Greedy thing. The ribs took it all in, filling itself to the . . . well, the ribs.

But they were so tiny. So thin. It couldn't have been an adult who died here. The wounds wouldn't have been as bad. An adult's bones would've been too thick to pinch through. These ribs were slim enough to prick through my skin, like the teeth of an animal might do—a fox or a wolf. I knew that it had to have been a child. Someone younger than any of us.

I had stepped on a brittle little girl. And she defended herself. All this, with nothing more than her bones. Now I'm being eaten from the inside out, because of it.

I found her. She should be thankful to me. There is no telling how long she's been laying in these woods. It's only by luck, her luck, that we traveled out this far, anyhow. This being the off-season, we needed to go deeper for the deer. Every year, the fawns thin out more and more, leaving us no choice but to come after them. And this is where it leads us. In the middle of nothing. I would've said this territory hadn't been touched in ages, if it wasn't for her. I wish she would've kept it secret.

Half of her skeleton was under the ground, the other half prodding up from the dirt. She must not have been happy with her burial, pulling herself back up for a better one. Her bottom jaw was still under the soil, a sparse tooth here and there peering up from the ground. She had been eating the earth. Grass had taken over, growing up through the eye sockets. Mother Nature wanted to seize her child, the grass working like green fingers trying to drag the skull back down into the dirt.

Her ribs only wanted to grab me, in hopes of getting my attention. Now that she had it, she wanted me to help her, somehow. There was an openness to those eyes. It was easy to look in deep, and find the girl still yearning within.

She'd had green eyes. I could almost see them. Lively green eyes, begging to fill those sockets again.

I stood up, only to have her rib cage come with me. She didn't want to let go. I must have been the first person she had touched in years, from the way she was clinging to me. When the rest of the group came to my aid, her skull looked up to us, mouth open wide in amazement at all these men. Begging for us to take her away. It had been simple enough to follow the formation of her skeleton. I started wanting to put her back together, flesh and all. See what she looked like when she'd been alive. A girl as young as that had to've been untouched. Which was unfortunate. For her sake.

But what made her remains so queer were the bones that didn't belong to her, scattered amongst her own. It could have been two skeletons, I thought at first—one possibly buried deeper into the ground. But no, there weren't enough bones to make up more than a fist. There was a clear difference between hands: thick fingers strewn about thinner ones, an adult's mingling with the child's. There were extra shards two sizes too large to fit into the puzzle of herself, all piled in her lower abdomen. Where the belly had been.

A joke rose up from one of the other men. Something about her liking me, wanting me to take her back to town.

A city-boy like you would have me all to your own, young man.

We laughed at her. Another fellow asked her if she'd want to come home with me, prodding her skull with the nose of his rifle, as if to sniff her hair. A little pressure just underneath the upper jaw, and he had pried her out from the grass's hold—the rip of it sounding like tendons stretching apart. The hooks of her lower jaw were left poking up from the dirt. He brought her skull up to my face, until I was eye-to-eyeless-eye with her—shredded grass spilling out from her sockets. The skull, mouthless now, speechless for good, rocked unevenly on the nozzle of this fellow's rifle, woozily teetering side to side.

Silly country girl, we all laughed. *See what happens when you leave us men behind?*

I had been chuckling enough to break the coagulating blood on my leg, the wounds peeling back their fresh red lips to laugh along with the rest of us. To keep that punchline striking, hitting and hitting until we couldn't stop laughing, had we tried—in a whim, I lessened the space between her and me, bringing the rifle to my chest until I was kissing this toothless child. *See what you get when you peck at me, you silly country girl? You get a peck back.*

When our lips met, whether anyone else could feel it or not, a certain wind had chosen to blow through right then, filling her entire skull. As the air blew through her eye sockets, she could've been a seashell at my ear. But no sound of the ocean inside of her, no. Not in this country girl, who probably never saw a body of water larger than her bathtub. Instead, that gust gave me an ill-wind that I still can't explain. It sounded so hollow inside, like a cavern, as if there were more emptiness to that skull than it could contain. A sound rolling and rolling through her cranium, yearning for more. A hunger that would never find its fill.

It kept blowing through my ears even after I dropped her to the ground.

Night was crawling over these woods, just waiting to seep through. Before too much longer, we would be in the dark. Camp needed to be set up, my leg tended to. Giving me my own tent was a good gesture. Kind, for sure. But now I realize it's because no one wanted to share a night with my dreams. I found myself in a cornfield. She was there, the girl, cropping up from the corn, her hair tangled into the stalks. Something in me needed to see the skin over her skull, to find those eyes where they belonged. But somehow, she was always at a distance from me. No matter how long I ran, she kept far away—until I was unable to catch my breath.

Giving up, I tried to stop. I was ready to lay down, but my feet wouldn't allow it. They kept running, pushing me through the corn; the stalks slapping against me, smacking me in the face. Panic erupted, my breath long since gone. I was going so fast that I couldn't even pick up the air slipping past me. I felt a pair of hands on my shoulders. A warmth brushed down my neck that had me turn around, only to see the girl's face at my ear. She was pushing me from behind. Her breath was dropping underneath my collar. I looked down to our feet, only I couldn't find them. Everything below our knees was a yellow blur. The ankles, the toes, the soles, the heels, all swallowed in flames.

When I looked ahead of me, there was such a wind in my eyes, I had to turn away or be blind forever. And there she was beside me. My country girl, pushing. There was such a calm to her. She was so close, I could see the corn reflecting in her green eyes. I found my own image inside there, as well. I simply stared at myself, staring back.

I hadn't even realized that she had been looking at me. She smiled because of it.

And almost as quick as her lips lifted into that grin, her lower jaw flapped back from the force of the wind, limply unhinging itself and falling away. Her cheeks waved through the air, slapping against her neck, her ears. The teeth from her upper gums began to unlatch, one dropping off after another, until her upper lip peeled up over her nose—revealing so much soft and open space.

As I watched all of this, her hands had moved from my shoulders to my neck. She wouldn't let me turn away from her. If I closed my eyes, her grip tightened around my throat. She kept me looking, as more and more of her ripped away.

The skull was an unwelcome friend to my lips. When we kissed again, this time by her doing, she pressed and pressed until I felt bone snag onto my cheeks. Until the empty cavity of her nose hooked mine. She swept me off my feet.

Tell me that's not a face to die for. Waking up to her this morning was a surprise. The green is rising up in her eyes again. You can see it around the edges of my leg, where the infection is worse. And look. Rosy red cheeks, she's blushing. I'd say she's a catch, if I had been the one who caught her. But as you can clearly see, she's the one who caught me. Everything below the knee. This country girl will have to come home with me. Now the only way to separate us is by saw. From the feel of it, they'll have to lop off a lot more than just my leg. I'd say, she's gone straight to my heart, by now, leaving me with a fever I can't keep up with. She'll dry my veins right out. All I'll pump is air, this ill-wind passing through, yearning for more. A hunger that will never find its fill.

correspondence of corpses

Mary Brown,
O Mary Brown.
Lost my husband
and banished from town.

Live in a shack
right next to the sea,
waiting for my husband
to wash up to me.

You'd think I penned the song myself, children, but no. Never had the knack at anything creative. Most I ever made with my hands were sweaters, knitted to fit Tom like skin. He'd need an extra layer out there at sea, so I was more than happy to dress him. Sewed his name into the collar, like all the wives say you should, whether you want to or not. *So you know, they say. Just in case some of him comes back while some of him doesn't.* These women were weaving an epitaph

into the very sweater they'd send their husbands off in—
which left my hands trembling, believe me. I couldn't even
thread the needle. What kind of wife sews her husband a
tombstone? Not me, no. Not to Tom, never. You could be sure
I did away with this *duty* of a fisherman's wife. If he was
heading out, well then—so was I. I went ahead and stitched
my name right alongside his, so the two of us would be there
together, stretched around his neck. And not with thread,
mind you. But a lock of my own hair. Cut enough off to spell
both of our names. Thomas and Mary Beth Brown, laced
into his navy blue sweater in red ringlets.

The closest thing to a necklace Tom ever wore was me.

You believe in things like that. You need to. When you
put as much of yourself into a sweater, those last words before the final goodbye would be all I'd hold on to until Tom
came back. My ears would grow deaf for him, holding their
breath on every other sound until the day they'd hear his
voice again. That was my oath.

But the words he gave me. I've sewn them into so
many sweaters since, wearing his promise around my heart,
my neck. He swore to me that on his return, he'd flash a
torch off the bow. Just for me, the moment he spotted land,
so that I'd know he was on his way home. Now, I had words
to hold him to. If his love rested in a flash of his torch, I'd
watch for it. He assured me there wouldn't be a star that
shined as bright as his light.

I'm sure the sky was jealous of him. No doubt in
league with the water, somehow—wasn't it? No doubt in my
mind, whatsoever.

Mary, Mary,
all old and scary.
Where did your husband go?

Went to the sea,
a fisherman was he,
but alive, you'll never know.

Isn't that what they're singing in town?

Well, isn't it? There have never been enough whispers about me, have there? With so many rhymes to go around, I somehow find my way into them all. You children will never understand. I wake up to eggs bursting over my windows, to field mice nailed to my front door by their tails. *And for waiting.* Having a heart full of patience, that's my cross to bear. Pray for your husband enough and it'll reach over oceans, but just make sure the right ears are listening. Otherwise, there's no telling who will answer back. So accuse me of anything other than love. If you do, well then, I dare you to explain why. Make me understand *why* I deserve this. Because I can't. I won't. What kind of mistake was it for me to pray as hard as I did? Just to bring him back. All I wanted was to see him again. To know. There was never a mention of him from other boats. No sign of wreckage. Nothing ever washed up.

It'd finally reached a year. This home had turned into a lighthouse burnt out on its hope.

And yet, there were words that I could muster from inside. I found them in the dregs, under the silt of my heart. I tossed them into the water like a fisherman's line. *Please,*

Tom. Please. Prayer found its way onto sweaters, the words reaching out as far as the sleeves. *Please, Tom. Please.* Prayer would catch him by the throat, hook into that sweater I had given him—which was really the only place where Thomas and Mary Beth Brown existed anymore. I'd use it to reel him back onto dry land. *Please, Tom. Please.*

This is what I hoped for, for years.

This is what made me infamous.

What tailored songs to my life.

Mary Brown,
she lives alone,
with no love around
to call her own.

Dug up a grave
with a caring hand.
A corpse she'd save
when she couldn't a man.

My plan for this Christmas is to sew a sweater for every child who sings of me. I'll stitch your rhymes into them, plucking out every hair on my head to do it, if need be, even if it leaves my scalp bare. I'll have the words wrapped around your heart as much as mine. And like a net, I'll squeeze your songs until they tighten around your tiny bodies.

One night, where sleep is a thin skin easily punctured, I woke up to a pounding on the front door. I expected to find another jellyfish on my welcome mat, or any other prank you children could imagine. In opening the door, the taste of pickled fish filled my mouth before I had the chance to shut it. Before me, on two feet, I found rot the likes of no disease. There was skin to it, yes, holding together a man that looked as if death had been goading him along for years, never allowing the lungs to stop or the heart to cease. Both of which were quite visible to me. But instead of pumping blood and breathing air, every pulse seemed to work off of water. Salt water.

And when I screamed, taking in a fair share of air to do it, somehow that sea had crept into me.

"Help, Mary. Please." His tongue shoveled up the words as best it could, but I couldn't get beyond the notion that he knew my name. This *thing* knew my name. What thread holding me to this earth was cut so quickly, that I accepted this guest as my own insanity, sewn together in a shoddy fashion.

"Thomas said you would understand."

I was only ten seconds into my madness. Only ten seconds deep in what could have been an eternity of drool and nightmares. But hearing *his* name triggered a softness. It dragged me back up to the surface of the situation, back to my front porch again. Three years after saying goodbye to Tom, and I heard his name spoken from someone other than me. Someone else's throat had said it. Or, at least, what throat was left. What only seconds before could just as well have caused my heart to stop, he let the blood flood it again.

Fresh air hadn't a chance in this house, ever since this man stepped through the front door. Rot was all the luggage he had, and the smell of it filled every corner of my home. I sat him down in the living room, lit a fire to warm him. It was then that light finally had a grasp of his body. Finding him under the moonlight had been horrible enough, but here was light giving attention to what stray meat still clung to the bone, a shadow under loose skin flickering every time his body shifted.

What explanation I caught was all I needed. There were many of them below. Waiting in a wet limbo. What brought him here was a voice, mine, somehow sinking to the depths and dragging him up. Simple as that. No magic, no fairy tales. Just a voice heard by hundreds. Hundreds of them, waiting.

Not two days later, he had a sweater. I hadn't sewn anything for anyone for years. I knew Tom's size as if it were my own, but this man was missing . . . shape, here and there. The lack of eyes, the thin hints of a mouth. Here I was, the mother to a corpse preserved on both salt and prayers. His name had been Roger.

A couple nights later, I heard a whispering of puddles. I wanted so much for it to be a dream, but I realized I'd stopped dreaming ever since nightmares began walking around my home. I followed the whispers until I reached the living room. What I found was less revolting than Roger, but blue in the skin and dead all the same.

Roger swiftly introduced me to Samuel.

After some time, it became necessary for me to sew their names into their sweaters, in hopes that I could keep my guests in order. Walter, Jonathan, Peter, Robert, Nicholas, Christopher. Names were all I had, really. The bones had begun to look alike, already, while the promises were all the same—

Tom's on his way home.
He'll be back soon, if not the next.
Just keep the prayers flowing, Mary Beth.
We need to hear the prayers . . .

It struck me that the lighthouse hadn't died after all. It's lit with a murkier bulb, one that Tom can't seem to get his eyes around.

He had been so anxious to leave, he practically forgot to even kiss me goodbye. When I caught him on the porch, he yanked his shoulder out from my hand and ran off without saying a word. Without even looking back at me. He, he wasn't even heading for the water. But to town. To that whore Lori Winters. You'd think he would have told me, wrote a note or fessed up before leaving, but no. He went ahead and left me to fester in this house. I knew he'd come back, sooner or later. He'd tire of sharing Lori Winters with the rest of the sailors in town and come home, where he belonged.

Wait. That's not true. That's not how it happened at all.

Mary Brown was an old lady
so jealous of the sea,
that when her husband begged her
she'd never leave him be.

So when he up and left her
a shovel did take she,
slapping it over his heart
until a beat there'd never be.

It's gotten so hard to know what's happened, anymore. I can't quite remember if Tom's still under the porch, or if he left with another woman, or if he's still out at sea.

You children will run by, toss an egg at my window. I'll be in bed, wondering why, *why do I deserve this?* Then I hear you singing, and it all comes back to me. Yes, Tom is at sea. Yes, I crushed Tom's skull years ago. Or, oh yes—How could I forget? All the dead sailors love their Mary. Whatever song I hear will remind me, and then my day is clear. Tomorrow can always change this. It all depends on the song, now, doesn't it? Tomorrow, Tom might only be a few rhymes away from me. Or not. It's not really my choice, now—is it? I leave that up to you children.

All I keep is a promise. A torch just above the water, so that I'll know he was on his way home. Brighter than any star, he said. Funny he didn't know that stars travel over such a great distance, that once you see its light, the star itself has already burnt out and died. At least I'll know where I left him. Or where he left me. How does it go?

I'm sorry, I've forgotten. It should be on a sweater here somewhere, I'm sure.

off-season spirits

The off-season's here, you can tell. The tourists have thinned out as much as the tan-lines. I should know. All my winters have been here. Never left once. Us locals pretty much live inside a skeleton come the end of summer, some carcass pecked free of all its insides. There'll be nothing around but the beach and boardwalk by December. A few shops will stay open year round, like us here. But business slims itself down after a spell. That's winter on the shore for you. Everyone just drifts off once the sun's gone. The waves wipe away the last few footprints by fall, smoothing the sand out until you'd think a foot had never come near it.

And all of the coast goes cold. The sand stiffens up so much, it's like you're walking over a corpse just to get to the water. That's how the beach feels, anyway. Dead. It's no wonder why everybody leaves.

It'll grow on you, though. Like barnacles to the pilings. After a while, you're paying it no mind. Best way to burn up some time, I find, is to come through here. If you're not believing me, you should give it a try. A dollar will let you walk through once. But once is enough. Trust me on that. We don't call this place haunted for our health, but for yours. Now, I don't tell many people this—but I'm swearing to you when I do—beyond these doors here, you're liable to find something mighty frightening. Sure, a lot of it's nothing more than pulleys and wire. Your normal scare-fare. But the building itself is an honest-to-God-possessed piece of property. Ocean's made sure of that, trust me. People who've passed through will swear by it. They'll even pay you not to go in.

(I get paid to say that part.)

Even if we closed for the winter, the place'd still be haunted. So, might as well keep it open for passersby. Like yourself.

Best company in a ghost town you're able to make are the ghosts, believe me. Look around. With the sun off 'til summertime, the sky'll never break a single cloud. You'd say it was soot. One look at it now and you'd never believe it ever could've been blue.

The only thing to get grayer than what's over your head is what's washing up at your feet. The water's always underneath you, that's for sure. It's got a grip on this town. Only way I've heard a local leave is by drowning.

I had an older brother stroll out at high tide and never come back. A young boy, like yourself. The salt in the air hadn't even toughened his skin yet.

Now he's a sponge for it.

I was nothing but a child myself, if I'm counting right. Pushing about, oh, yea-high. I was cut a few inches shorter than my brother, up until he gargled the air right out of himself. There had always been a race between him and me to reach six foot. That, or the bigger pecker. Since he had a year on me, he'd always brag about having the inches in his favor. But we'd wrestle over it every season. Come the end of summer, we'd stand back to back and measure each other, height-wise. Whoever was taller got the ruler first.

Six foot or six inches. The first to cross the finish line marked on the yardstick won a chance to ask out our shared summertime crush. It was the only fair shot either of us could think of, since our sights were knotted on the same mermaid from the boardwalk. You ever see one of those before? They only charge a quarter to look at her. In a fishbowl the size of a beach ball, she'd wave to the tourists—her limbs looking like seaweed rolling through the water. I'd always wave back, hoping she could pick me out from the crowd. There was always a ton of people, just watching her sit there on this little treasure chest the size of my thumb. They kept this torn red velvet rope in between her and the rest of us.

You'd have to squint hard if you wanted a good look at her. Most of the times, a good look was all you needed. She was so small, I could've held her in my palms if I cupped them, handling her like an oyster bearing its pearl.

A quarter a peek didn't make her a cheap date, though. By the end of summer, me and my brother had gone through all our allowance, which pretty much left us stranded from doing anything. He had to get this job at the local movie theater, which is closed now. It was down the boardwalk there, a few blocks over. Back then, it had been the biggest thing to wash up on this shore. Picture it: westerns instead of bingo. Cowboys instead of beach-combing.

Once business slowed down for the winter, they started to show skin flicks at night. Since I was so young, my brother would sneak me up into the balcony for all the late shows. No one else would be up there but us, having the entire stretch of seats for ourselves. We'd do just about anything we wanted to, from spitting cola onto the men masturbating below to swimming through our own pants. We would sit at opposite sides of the balcony and wait for the film to hit its peak. It wouldn't take long before our hands were below the belt, our eyes holding onto that screen like a life jacket in the tide. I'd just dive into the film, getting all in the movement of things. I'd lose sight of where I was, almost feeling like I was on-screen with all the movie stars. And the feeling would rise up in me. This warmth from my lower back. It would crawl up my spine until I thought I was growing right along with it, reaching heights so high I couldn't even have fit the screen.

Felt like I was some giant. That I could get out of this

town if I wanted to. Whatever was on the other side of this ocean was now just a step away, and I'd feel myself soar over it like I could feel myself soaring over the balcony. Those were the moments when I was the high tide, when I was a wave crashing on the people beneath me. I'd sink back into my seat, feeling everything else sink back into me. My old size, my old clothes. Me and my brother would just watch the rest of the film, keeping our pants at our heels the whole night.

After the movie was over, we'd go back to her. See her sitting in her bowl. The look in her eye would make you believe she'd been waiting for you the whole time you were gone. That's the draw, I guess.

She'd pull you into romance or the undertow. Mermaids are known for it.

To cut back on costs, we planned to propose together. Putting a lot of thought into it, we figured the two of us would wait in the alleyway out back on bent knee, counting down to closing time. I had the ring. Something I had whipped up on my own. It was this nickel-sized starfish, with a loop of pipe cleaner for her finger. I kept it in a clamshell already shucked, while my brother held a bouquet he had made out of kelp.

You figure, if you're going to do it once, then you got to do it up real nice. We'd even chipped in for a fish tank, thinking we'd need it for the honeymoon.

But beyond those bases, we didn't know what else there was to cover, really. Whether some guy was going to haul her out in her bowl and toss her into the sea, or if she was going to come hopping out on her own—we hadn't the foggiest.

I never remember our hearts sounding so loud before. Between us, there were wedding bells chiming in our chests. But when two legs came walking out the back door, some forty-year-old woman on top, you could've heard a heart-break so heavy, you would've thought a tidal wave had just slapped our backs. At first, I wasn't going to believe it was her. Her tail was hooked on a coat hanger hung over her shoulder. The shine to her scales looked more like sequins from up close. There was a cigarette where she always had a smile before, smoke trailing out from her mouth where bubbles used to be.

Taking one good look at us, she brought that smile up. It was a little bigger than I had remembered it. There was some lipstick still there, rubbed off on her teeth. You could see the summer was doing a job on her skin, wrinkling it up just like all the rest of the people here. Even she couldn't beat it.

We ended up running all the way home, never mentioning that mermaid to each other ever again. After that, my brother took a distrust to marine life. One night, he said he was going out for a little beach-combing. But he walked right up to the ocean, saying to hell with the sand. He wanted to have a word with the waters. He got a mouthful of it instead.

Out of superstition, I guess, my mother kept a light on by the window, marking our house for years. It was the only light you'd see for miles along the shore. I could walk the coast and never worry about losing my way at night.

She had hoped the same for my brother.

It took me to turn fifteen before she let me get a job on the boardwalk. It didn't seem right to her that I'd want to get near the water after what happened. In her mind, working at the haunted house was the best job I could get. I'd have enough ghosts around me to keep me away from the shore. It'd be a reminder why the beach is better off-limits.

The way I looked at it was, now I had family on both sides of the sea.

For ten years now, I've cut a dollar or so out from every paycheck, saving myself the money for the boardwalk. A quarter a visit makes her a cheaper peek than the women at the peep shows. It's sort of the same thing, anyways. I don't mind. When everything else dies in the winter, she's still there for me—breathing a little bit of life back into this town. The same rope is between us, just a little more ripped in places. They don't line up for her like they used to, so I can just dip my hands down my pants. Never bother a soul. She's so far away from me, I don't think she even notices. Maybe she just doesn't care. But I dive in, and look hard for that feeling that used to come so quick.

But I never find myself growing up, reaching that height that used to lift me out of this town. Now, I just shrink down. Small enough to fit inside the fish bowl with her.

I married that mermaid whether she knows it or not. My big brother was my best man, still the same age he was when he left. Got hitched right here in the haunted house. All of our guests had either drowned or lived underwater already, making for a lively crowd. Pulleys and wire. Mechanical ghosts and real ones. Fish cutting up a rug with rubber skeletons and it was all one hell of a picture.

Me and that mermaid are going to take our honey-moon into the ocean. No plane tickets, no need to pack. The two of us are just going walk out. First up to my knees, then up to my chest, finally up to my lungs with a salty drink.

This place is going to be our home. There isn't a day that goes by without a pulley snapping or a wire slipping off its track. When I go to fix whatever's broken, I'll find my brother there instead. The rubber mask of a phony ghost will give way to his face, the wires become a part of him. He says he's been here all along. They all have been. The place became a home to those from town who drowned years back. Where else were they going to go? The locals who feel like visiting family stop by whenever they like. They're usually the only ones coming in this time of year. It's a reminder that our lives have more stock in the ocean than on ground. We're a floating people. Our heritage holds itself together with seaweed rather than roots. It's stronger than any limb a family-tree could find on dry land.

poor man's mermaid

The waters have been good to me today, by God. I tell
you, those currents went ahead and answered my prayers not
a moment too late.

It's you, you and that skin. You thought you were blue
enough to slip right under my nose, didn't you? You thought
you could play a trick on me and see if I wouldn't notice. But
no ma'am. No way that'll ever happen while I'm under here.
I tell you, underneath this pier—all I have are what those

currents drag up for me. The same currents, God bless them, that brought you to me. I'll spot the tiniest ripples pass by— I'll wait for them, you see. And that's when I know there's something coming in from below. But never something like this, nope. They never did bring me a beauty like you. Bottles for sure. Maybe, if I'm lucky, a bag or an empty popcorn box. But never a beauty like you.

But I've been praying at night, you see. I've been praying so hard, my teeth start to hurt. I guess someone just heard me asking enough to think that maybe it was about time that I got what was coming my way. And here you are. Straight out of the water, right here to me. If that's not fate answering, then whatever it is, God bless it for listening.

Look at you.

I've been trying to keep things neat for this. Believe me, it's hard with the tide sneaking in the way she does when I'm not looking. She's the riley kind, that ocean. That's for sure. Just as much as she'll hand me something, she'd take it all away when my back's turned. I have to hide the important things farther up the shore, behind those poles over there, where she can't find them. I even dig me up a hole now and then and bury the stuff like it was in some kind of treasure chest. Just like in the books. I should even make up a map and everything. Just for the fun of it, just like they did in those books.

You got to think about these things when you're down here. Word gets out and it's all gone. Everything I get from her, she sweeps it right back up again. Don't ask me how. She's got this way of listening I can't figure.

It's getting harder than it used to be. Hiding. 'Cause every day those currents are coming in closer, taking a little bit more of that beach. It's like she's moving in somehow, right from underneath me. Looks the same, sure. But that's because she's got the smarts to take just enough that I don't notice. Until one day, where I'm standing on sand, I've got water rushing over my feet. No one else can even make heads or tails from the way it was yesterday, but that's because they stay up there all the time. No one comes down here.

I just wish they could see what's going on, that's all. I mean, I just want them to know what's happening under their noses. Because I hear kids walking up there, I hear families. And, and that scares me. I don't want anyone to get hurt.

I tell you—if no one's gonna do anything about it, this ocean is going to swallow it all whole someday.

Would you listen to me? I'm spouting off like I just got my first mouth or something. I'm sorry. I really don't do this a lot, don't worry. I admit it—I start acting up when I get excited over things. But can you blame me for getting a little excited? Can you? Nah, I don't think so. I don't think so.

It's funny though, 'cause one thing always reminds me of something else. You ever get that? That ever happen to you? You're going to get a kick out of this one—okay? When I was in school, they used to call me by this old poet's name. I know it sounds corny. I mean, I can't even remember what the guy's name was. But they did it because they said I'd always get real excited about the small things. Whatever that meant. Passionate. They thought I was passionate, because I'd get all worked up over the small things while no one else cared. Just like this guy. Can't remember his name though. Yeah, I should. But I can't think of it. He was supposed to be a real ladies' man, which I liked. Being called his name and all. 'Cause that way then people'd think I was some kind of ladies' man too. I tell you, anything to get the ladies.

You cold? You feel cold to me.

You know, I had an idea that you'd be out there. Let it be said that I had my eye open since day number one. Looking out there, trying to find you under all that. Keep goals for yourself, they say. So my goal was to find you. Took me a while, yeah. But look at me now, you know? Look at how it paid off. In spades is how I see it. Paid off in spades.

I can take you back to the very day my father brought me here, up there. All the way to the end of the pier. He helped me climb up to the top railing while all he had to do was just lean over. Like he was going to jump off or something. He'd have me wrap my hands around his arm and lift me over like he was some kind of crane or something. Both of my feet would just take off from the pier and he'd call me his catch of the day. Sometimes he'd get all funny on me and start kidding around, just kidding around and holding me over the water, saying stuff like, *"We gotta throw this one back, he's no keepa. We gotta throw this one back."* And I'd laugh and close my eyes if I looked down, and I'd hold on to that arm with both of my hands and laugh and start to cry and then he'd bring me back over the railing.

I never let go of him, never. Even on the pier, I never let go. He'd bring me back over and lean himself onto that railing, getting quiet all of a sudden. And just look forever at the water going by. I think that's why we went, 'cause he'd always get caught up in the water. Never said a word to me once that happened. No, it'd just be real quiet with the seagulls . . . seagulls over my head and all he'd do was look. He'd turn just enough that an ear'd be reaching out for the water, like he was listening to it. What, he wouldn't say, until he'd bring up his other hand and point to the currents. And he'd say to me without even moving an eye my way, *"They got mermaids out there, son. Most beautiful creatures alive and a man be blessed if he was ever to spot one."*

Every time. That's what he always said to me, never fail. I guess I just remember that. It was just one of those things you did with your father when you were little, you know? It was just one of those things. I made a goal for myself that I'd bring my boy here when we got the chance. To show him the water from over there. Yeah. But they say boys grow up fast, though. Faster than you'd think. Quicker than you can feed them, that's for sure. Every mouthful another inch up in the legs.

Anyways. I don't want to think about that anymore.

You got this hair. I want you to know I really think you have beautiful hair. It holds to you. It kind of clings on and doesn't want to let go, does it? Not that I can blame it or anything. I mean, if I had the chance, I bet I'd probably do the same—no doubt about it. I was just noticing it. How it, how it wants to protect you from everybody else. Like your own blanket to keep you safe. I can understand why it wants to do that. I don't blame it.

You mind if I, if I pull it back? Just out of your face?

It's hard to see you with all your hair in the way. Just out of your face, that's all.

Look at that. Will you take a look at that? I'm telling you, it's that skin. It's the, I think it's the palest skin I've ever seen. You touch it, and you get this shiver over your back. Like it's frozen, like it's made out of ice. I touch it, and the air in my lungs freezes over. If the men up there knew you were out under the waters, *if they knew*, they'd throw their poles down and jump right off the pier. Not even give it a second's thought, I'm sure of it, they'd leave everything behind for one look at that face. And those eyes . . . You've got these eyes that are as, as glassy as a couple of jellyfish. A couple of jellyfish left on a beach of pale skin.

And they're looking at me. Why would you ever blink when you've got the whole world right in front of you? I'd never do it if I had you in front of me all the time. I don't think I could. Why would I?

I'd wash the sand from your hair with the ocean itself. I'd tuck you in under a blanket of the high tide. I'd do anything to touch that skin. To kiss those lips and taste the salt soaked in 'em, I'd spend every sand dollar there ever was on this beach. I'd do it for you. To have those eyes looking into mine, one ocean staring into the other and never a blink in between—that's beauty. That's something you've got that says something a hundred times louder than anything I've ever said. To look forever and never hide those eyes, not from anyone, that's something no one's ever done for me.

So I'd do it for you.

I don't know. It makes me sad thinking about everything else. About . . . Thinking about how people just don't look anymore. I mean, coming down here was like disappearing, you know? Now no one seems to notice. They just don't look down here, that's all. They look over it. The pier keeps everyone looking in the other direction, to the people over there burning themselves silly. They've got nothing on you, that's for sure. They don't know what being beautiful really is.

I mean, will you take a look at them? They're trying to burn their skins right off. Why would you ever want to do something like that? You stay under the sun long enough and you get these wrinkles running all up and down your body. These, these splits running through your skin. Have you ever seen someone like that? Have you ever had to touch that stuff? Those cracks make their skin all dry to your fingers. It's like you're not touching someone anymore—you're hugging an old jacket. I tell you, holding onto someone like that, you feel like they're gonna crumble right through your arms. You don't need that, that's no good. They're coming here for all the wrong reasons. They're rubbing trouble all over themselves so they can bake under the sun—making me feel like I'm the ugly one. You think that's fair? You think that's right of them? Makes them look beautiful, they say. Better than you, is what they're thinking. I'm not angry about it, I'm not. It's just not right for them to keep thinking like that. It's not right.

I mean, how could they understand what's out there in the water when they're trying to blind themselves? Looking into the sun like that. They'd never understand it. No one's ever been able to understand that beauty's not something you can burn into your body—it's something that swims to you. It's something that you hear from in between the currents.

I knew you were out there. I knew and that scared people. All this time they've tried dragging the years right out from under me, sweeping everything I've had right out from under my nose. They're making me hide my life. Making me bury it so deep, I need a map when I want to find it again. Where does that leave me? Under the shadows? Under this pier? I've had to say to myself over and over again, if I'm supposed to wait this one out, I will. I'll do it. And you see what it's done to me? I've had to live like some troll from those nursery rhymes, waiting for so long the barnacles are grabbing at my skin.

What have I got left then?

So I prayed. You never think the right thing to do is just stop holding your breath and ask. That's when it hits you. That's when everything comes so clear in your head, it's like hearing yourself speak for the very first time. Well, I heard it. I heard what my father was listening for. It brought me back a whole lifetime later. It left me under the shadows wishing so hard, my eyes felt like they were gonna slip out from their sockets like oysters from the shell.

That's all I could do. That's all I've been able to do for so long now.

I want to hold on to you. You've been laying there all this time and I can't help myself from thinking it. Would you hold me? I want to hold on to you. Would you hold me?

Here. I'll help you.

And there you were, you know? Just like that. Washing up on the shore. Right here to me. With your skin as blue as the ocean you came from, your hair as wet as a nest of eels— you answered my prayers. After gutting this ocean clean, there isn't nothing that'd be able to take you away from me now. I promise. No matter how far that ocean can sneak up on me, swallowing as much sand as she can stomach, she'll never be able to find you now. Because I'll have a map leading me straight to you every time I see the coast is clear.

Hey. Make a break for the bathroom while you still can,
boy. There are worse things than what's under your bed, believe me. Instead, if I were you, I'd worry over what comes
creeping out from my own crotch. Don't want Daddy to find
your bedspread all stained, now. Do we? Not when our birthday's just around the corner. Better keep them sheets as
white as your teeth. Couldn't cover a cavity like that under
your blanket but for so long. Lips have got to give, sooner or
later, no matter how stiff the starch.

That dried patch of pee-pee is going to spoil a year's worth of potty training.

It'd be a shame for your father to think he's raised a bed-wetter for a boy. Piss isn't anything to be proud of, especially when it's been puddling up in your mattress for years. What's the matter? Bathroom too far for you? Don't tell me you couldn't reach the toilet in time. You're not even giving it a shot. You just let it all seep through your tighty-whities, getting your legs to gutter the flow. That rush will leave a rash before too long, believe me. Keep this pissing up, and the insides of your thighs will itch so much, such sore sandpaper skin, you'll rub them together until they're raw.

You're wearing down your knees to the bone, boy. Without legs, you'll never make it to the bathroom. So go on, then—one foot in front of the other.

Daddy's wrapping you up a bed pan for your birthday, I saw him. Rather than tucking you in with a new teddy bear, you'll be sleeping with a plastic sack to piss in. How about a catheter for your sweet seventh year? Beats a baseball bat, now. Doesn't it? You'll be the only boy under sixty on this block to have one. What a way to make friends with the old folk, hey? Get in with the geriatrics, all 'cause you can't keep your sheets clean. Got to keep under the covers, no matter how tight your kidneys grip. Got to play tug-of-war with your own wee-wee. All 'cause the birthday boy here is afraid of the dark. Right? That hallway's holding enough shadows to hide a whole hell of a lot of things. Lord knows just what. Simply thinking about what might be out there, slipping around in that swarthiness, coiling up in the corner and just

waiting to strike—*why, you forget about your groin.* Can't remember why you've kept your legs clamped together for so
long, until . . .

Oh my, there it goes! Dam's cracked, here comes the
flood . . .

Your toes will be welcoming the incoming tide in no
time, boy. And what wetness starts off tickling will only turn
into an itch before too long. Let this piss dry into your skin
and you'll never be able to scratch it back out.

Believe me.

How do you think I feel down here? Never dared to
look under your bed, now. Did you? Well, I don't mind. I was
calling this home well before you moved in. Before you were
even born, boy. I bet. Can't say how long I've been down
here, but I know there were at least fifty boys shuddering
under those covers before you. Maybe more. It all leads up to
the same thing, really. A downpour. Right on top of me. The
people who sold your father this house were smart enough to
slide your bed right into the corner, here. Otherwise, he
would've found a fracture in the floorboards. There's a hole
down here. Did you know that? Nothing but a shaft fit for a
little boy's body. Got an opening as thin as your urethra.

I'm not asking for company, don't worry. Tight enough
down below, as is. It just leads me to believe that I'm to
blame for your bed-wetting. Am I? You can tell me, I won't
mind. Wouldn't be such a chore to get up from under your
blanket, if you thought you'd have a safe break to the bathroom, I know.

Didn't even realize it myself. When this was my room,

my bladder would force me out of bed. Get me to the door, but not much farther. The bathroom was too far down the hall, you see? I couldn't walk all that way without stepping into some shadow. The carpet was covered in them, the floor all puddled. Put a foot down and there's no telling how deep my toes would go. I'd never make it. But for a little boy like me, with enough milk bottled into my belly to fill the toilet bowl two times over, I needed to get rid of it, somehow. Puckering up my knees only worked for a few minutes before my thighs would start to sweat, making things all the more slippery for my kidneys. But I wasn't about to become a bed-wetter, no. Not with my father. Not with my birthday on the way. I needed to save my sheets, somehow. To save my hide.

I'd come over to the corner here, pull up on the rug just enough to flash them floorboards. Lift up that lip for a big smile. Went to the bathroom right there. Figured it would run right through the cracks and that would be it. Never have to think about it again. The wood would sponge it all up. After I was done, all I'd need to do was roll the carpet back over. Never happened. Nobody'd know. Lips are sealed.

Every night, I'd try to hold it in. I'd try to make it to the morning, I swear. But if I couldn't, if I absolutely had to let go, I'd head over to the corner. Aim for the same spot. Once the flow got going, I'd just close my eyes and squeeze. Force it all out. Then run back to bed. Never happened. Nobody'd know. I didn't even need to look down. I could tell where to piss simply by the sound of the splashing. If the rattling seemed too tight, that was where the wood was still solid. But if the piss muttered up in a puddle, more muffle than rumble, that's where I'd fire. The wood had sopped up so much of me, that after a while, it started to stain. The floor darkened. Getting thicker each night. Coming from me. I couldn't look into it, anymore. Had to squat over the corner, now. Straddle that shadow. Feed it more.

I'd get so scared walking over here. The wood had become so soft around the edges. If I stood too close, my toes would sink into the floor. Couldn't stand but so near for fear of falling in. No telling where I'd end up. No telling how deep I'd go down. But a boy's bladder isn't built for going to bed. Is it? Won't hold more than a handful of milk before you need to pee again. That sack inside yourself, that itty-bitty little baggy—it's tiny enough to get you on your feet every hour.

Didn't think you drank that much *milk—did you, boy?* *Well* . . . Seemed to me the bed above had sprung a leak. I'd been minding my own business down here for years, trying to sleep myself, when all of a sudden, I get this drip tapping me on the forehead. Seeming to say, *plink, plink, time to wake up. You've got a new roommate* . . .

And then I felt that familiar burn of urine. You know that prickle you get on your thigh when you shake yourself off a little too hard after tinkling? Something along the lines of acid splashing on your leg, I'm sure. A little dab will do you. Well, I was stinging all over. Down from my scalp, your *accident* then trickles onto my dried lips. Such chapped slivers of skin, really. Cracked enough for your fluids to flow right through, these ditches in my lips leaving my mouth without much say in the matter. So, down the hatch with your winky-tink. *And let me tell you*, I simply love that salty flavor of freshly squeezed kidneys. Oh boy, my tongue leaped on you like a root reaching out for water. You quenched this withered weed down once again.

Thanks so much.

If it wasn't for bed-wetters like you, I'd have shriveled up by now. Guess I'm blessed to be preserved on piss. Nothing more than a salted six-year-old boy, really. Years worth of urine have peeled away most layers of my skin. Rinsed the hair clear off my head, one wet clump at a time. Nearly left me blind, taking so much of it in the eye. My retinas have been chewed through, worn down by that constant rush. Thought I never got to see the sunlight from down here. Didn't realize it trickles down to me, night after night. Yellow beams burning right through my eyelids.

Not that I have much to look up at now, anyway.

All I see is the underside of your mattress, a new stain spreading through every evening. Like clouds forming over my head. And it always rains. Always showers down on me.

I fell into a well worn down by my own urine. Slipped right through the floorboards and never climbed out. My father thought I ran away. I never left my room. My birthday had been just around the corner. Closer than the bathroom. My father had promised me a teddy bear. Something to make the dark not so lonely when I got tucked in. I never got to unwrap it. But I've tried to make friends. Just wanted somebody to talk to. Maybe help me, maybe toss down your wee-wee and pull me up. But the only pals I have down here are your bladders. You kids have kidneys that keep me enough company. When they start blabbering, there's no plugging them up. And believe me, boy. I'm all ears down here. You can't hide your bed-wetting from me, if you tried. Wrapping those legs together won't help keep your secrets.

So just go on then. Fill me in. My lips are sealed, I promise.

a step off from fathering

Wake up, Henry. I need to talk to you.

Come on, son. There's not much time left for me to call you that, anymore. You want to spend it all under the sheets? Hmm? You want to take what's left of your stepfather's time by hiding from him? That's not really fair. Is it, Henry? You don't want me to leave with my feelings hurt, do you?

I know you can hear me, Henry. And I'm sure you know I've been sitting here for a while now. All I want is to have a little last-minute father-son chat. One for the road. Your mother's been awfully nice to give me ten minutes to apologize. And then I'm on my way. So. How about you come out and talk with me. That sound so bad?

Henry. You think you could do that for me?

There are one of two ways this can happen, Henry. If you're going to force me to give you an ultimatum, I will allow a total of thirty seconds to share with you your options. I am going to have this conversation with you regardless of you wanting it or not, so you can either—

A. Come out from underneath your Star Wars blanket and face me like Luke Skywalker would. Or—

B. Stay where I can't see you and listen to what I have to say, anyways.

You like those options, Henry? Not much room to pick and choose, I know. Decisions like these can leave you in a tight corner, where it's just going to get harder and harder to breathe. Just don't blame me if you're feeling a little stuffy under there, all right? Don't tell your mother I didn't give you the chance. She's been kind enough to give me this much time with you alone. Don't think I appreciate you forcing me to fill it up on trying to get you to look at me.

That's no way to treat your stepfather, especially after all the things he's tried to do for you.

I've tried to do for you. Jesus, would you just please come out? I'm talking in the third person now, I sound like an idiot. It's hard enough doing this. You could at least try to make it a little easier on me. What, you think I was going to be a pro at this or something? You were the first, Henry. First son I ever had to deal with. Chances are I won't be having another anytime soon, so consider the rest of the world lucky. Is that the way you want me to feel?

How do you want me to feel, Henry? I can say I'm sorry again for all the bad things I've done to you and your mother. That I was the mean one and the two of you were saints all along. I can say those things to you, Henry. I can keep saying them until my jaw drops, if that's going to make it all better for you.

But I don't think that's what you want from me. Is it? I get a feeling you would want the truth. You really want to know what divorce means? Well, I can tell you. I can share with you all the amazing things that go on between a mommy and a stepdaddy when little Hanky isn't around. All the wonderful talks they have about their baby boy, would you like that? If I was to tell you, maybe, one of these days when you're older—when you have children of your own— you'd look back at tonight and thank me for doing this.

Know that everything I have done to you, I have done *for* you, in hopes that you would learn something from it. None of this has ever been for my benefit. This right now, this might be the biggest lesson a father—stepfather—could teach a boy like you. Ready?

You know what it's like to need something? Not want something, but *need* something, Henry. Remember last Christmas when I said you wouldn't be able to open your presents until you told me what the old saying, "don't look a gift-horse in the mouth" meant? Well, the point to all that was to teach the difference between *needing* something and *wanting* something. Because you needed pajamas, whether you wanted them or not. And you wanted a new Star Wars toy, when you had no need for one. I don't know if you ever fully understood what I was trying to get across to you then.

So here's a different way of looking at it. Your mother needed me. She had you to worry about all on her own, and that scared her. Your real father left her, left you, which meant she had no way of supporting you. She didn't know how she was going to put food on the table, which is a very scary thing for a mother. I'm sure one day, you'll worry over it, too. All adults do. Because sometimes, the things we need—we just can't get them for ourselves. Sometimes, people need the help of others to get those things. And as fate would have it, that's when I showed up, Henry. And all of your troubles went away. Poof, just like that.

Sounds like a happy ending. Doesn't it? Remember how happy we were when we had all the things we needed? You got that blanket, and you had food on the table. And that meant, we were all happy.

The trouble was, Henry, your mother never wanted me. That's key, remember that. There was so much cluttering her mind, that when I came along, she mistook her need for love—which are two very, very different things.

I can teach you a lot, son. About wants and needs and a whole bunch of other squiggly feelings that crawl up inside you. But what I can't teach you a thing about is love. I don't know a thing about it. I swore I did. It got me to the altar and it brought me here, Henry, but I can't rightfully say it's love anymore. Because within three years, this feeling I had inside of me, which I would have sworn to you was love—it curdled. It festered in this house so quickly I would have mistaken it for someone's dog dying underneath our porch.

Let me give you an example. You were three when me and your mom got married. You were so young, it must be hard to remember the wedding. Such a small head like yours can't hold every memory just yet. But I remember taking you out in the backyard, just you and me. I'd pick you up and toss you into the air. You were the lightest thing to me. You would leave my hands for hours, only falling back into them when the clouds would let you go. But I'd stay down there, waiting for you to come back. A smile firm on those lips, as firm as my hands around you. And that laugh, Henry. When you were younger, you had a laugh that would never stop. It would land on me before you did. It was in those moments that I felt so lucky, like I had been given the greatest gift a man could have. A family. I had a family in my hands.

And I didn't want to ever see it go.

Do you know why we always went to your mother's parents for the holidays? You never asked about my parents. Did you ever get curious about who they were? Let me tell you. My parents were not like your mother's. No, mine had problems—firm issues to be dealt with. But they never were, and they have me to show for it. Now, adults call those consequences. I was a consequence, Henry. Adults and children alike don't look too kindly on consequences. For a boy like you, a consequence is something you get when you leave your toys out and I take them away. For adults like my mom and dad, a consequence is me. They didn't think about another kind of thing called responsibility. And when I came around, they had that to deal with, too. And they didn't do such a good job at it, Henry. I'll leave it at that.

That's why I've tried to teach you about responsibility. That's all. That's all I've been trying to do here. Because, you see, your mother and real father were the same as my parents. And you were their consequence. Your real father didn't know how to handle the responsibility, and he left. So then I came, because I knew what it felt like to be in your shoes. I didn't want to see you go through the same things I did, so I figured you could learn from me, from all of us, and right a wrong that could run over generations.

We're more alike than you might think, Henry. You and me, we're two of the same. Remember that when you get to the altar.

Hey. How about you come out here and give me a hug. I'd much rather talk to you than Darth Vader, so why don't you just come out from under there. Just talk to me. I promised your mom I wouldn't make you do anything you didn't want to do yourself, but I could really use this, Henry. It would make me real happy to see you one last time. Because after this, I'm gone. Your mom doesn't want me here anymore because she thinks I've been hurting you all this time. And that's not true. That's far from the truth.

Isn't it, Henry? You know I always looked out for you. Above everybody else. I've always been the one who said you were going to grow up to be something special. I said it, because I was going to make sure of it. You didn't hear anyone else promise that. The recipe for a good man isn't so hard to follow, you know? You just need the right ingredients. And what do you start with, Henry? Responsibility. Right. That's the secret, right there. Add that and the rest is a cakewalk. You want to know why I took away your toys? There's your answer. One word. I'd wait for those moments, hound on them, just so we could start the lessons off easy and early. You want to know why I had you stay inside while the other kids played in the street? Because responsible children take out the trash before they play, they make sure they have a clean house before leaving it. And Henry, this house was never clean. I made sure of that. I wanted to see you take on some responsibility, take it by the reins and ride it on into fatherhood. Because there are still a lot of boys outside, Henry. They're in the street right now, at ten at night, all day, all morning, just waiting to get hit so they don't have to face any of life's consequences. So, if you ever want to know why I laid a hand on you, you'll have every reason waiting right here, right on the other side of your blanket. Because it's in this house, Henry. You think it's me, but no, it's not. It's everything you're too afraid to face. You've got to be the man of the house now, your mother's made sure of that. You better start looking it all right in the eye or there's going be a whole chain of little boys growing up in this family. It'll run right on through your son and onto his and on and on and on, until you stop hiding underneath there and start acting like a real man.

I tell you what. For every baby you have while I'm still alive, I'll send them a blanket to remember me by, so that they'll know who's looking out for them. Is that what you want? You want to make me out to be just like your real father? Or do you want me to treat you with some respect? I've always given you options, Henry. Your dad never did that.

There's a final one for you. To grow on.

Boy, oh boy. Talk about a mouthful. Maybe it is easier to chat with good old Mr. Vader after all. I'll quit with the lessons. No point in leaving on a sour note. You know I'm only looking out for you, that's all. No matter what your mother is going to say, know that I only had your best intentions in mind. When the two of us would be in the backyard, and I'd toss you up in the air—it was those times that I realized how frail a child can be, how weak. And I never dropped you once, Henry. You were an egg to me, a shell so soft my hands never forgot the feel.

Either when I'd hug you or do some disciplining.

So. What do you say? How about a hug right now? I think I deserve at least a goodbye. A handshake, if I'm lucky. Come on, Henry. Why are you doing this to me? I want a good look at you before I go. My time's almost up here, your mom is going to come in any minute now. She'll tell me I'm going to have to leave, and I don't want to do that until you say goodbye to me. That's all I need from you, Henry. All I need is to hear you say, "Goodbye, Dad," and then I'll be on my way. It's important for me to know that you're going to be okay, that everything's going to be just fine. You're the only one I can get that from right now, Henry. You. Not your mom or anyone else. Just you. Because, right now, nothing else matters. It's all gone for me, everything I built myself up on for the last three years. My life ends the second I walk out this door.

But if I hear you say just one word to me, then I'll know everything is going to work out. If you just give me that, please, then it won't be so hard on my own. Because then I'll know that you still love me. I'll know that I was doing the right thing all along. For you, me, and the rest of this family—I will have taught you how to be a man. Please, Henry. All I'm asking is for you to look at me. One word, Henry. And then I'm gone. That's it, that's all. Like magic, I'll disappear for good. You want me to say I'm sorry? I can. I will. Just let me hear you. Please, son.

For your stepdad.

. . . What? I've got a minute left. Just give me one more minute. One more. We're finally starting to talk man-to-man, here.

milking cherry

I wouldn't pay it mind, if I were you. A scar like that might move in on your fun, get in the way of us having a good time. If I just pinch the shades a little, it'll be as if you never saw a thing. Okay? Nothing more than a freckle, anyway. Don't worry yourself over it, darling. It isn't even there.

See? I can't even remember where it was anymore. How 'bout you?

You got some nosy hands for yourself—you know that?

What're you looking for back there? All right. If you're so curious for it, then why don't we play a little game of hide-and-go-seek? I'll hide my marks and you come find them. Sound like fun? There's more where that one come from. I got them all over. I doubt I could show you them all.

Here, give me a finger. You feel that? That's my first. Others found more painful places to lay, but this one I'll remember most. It's more the shame that slipped in under the skin than the knife, that's still with me. Most men never care to notice. Not when it's their hour. Not even when their time's up. Some though, the bitter types—they find those scars and see an opportunity. They'll pull out their own knives while I go pull open the curtains, letting all that sun in so they can see where there's a free space. But it was this one, my first, that paved the way for all the others. Once that one laid down, the others followed right along. 'Cause once you're marked, your body's not good for anything else. I'm a cutting board for these men. That's all.

If you want to leave a notch, then you put your money near the window sill. Once I count your last dollar, then you quit cutting. You hear me? That's how I handle myself. If you don't like it, then there's the door and there goes your hour. You're not going to find many ladies in here who're gonna give you this much, not as much as I'm willing to hand over. But it's gonna cost you. My thighs are all full. Back's more like a blackboard someone forgot to erase. Breasts look like they've been chewed on. So, let's see. That leaves you a little bit 'round the stomach. There's still some space along there. Or my shoulders. They're clear, but they'll cost you another dollar. I keep my neck open for those who can afford it. All right?

You just stay away from my face. That's where I draw my line—you hear? I'm not going to look myself in the mirror and see you stuck with me whenever I do. The others I cover when I step out that door. The only time I deal with them is in here—you got me? They don't exist unless I see them, and that only happens when I'm in this room. Outside, I'm a clean woman. I keep a free face for my life, thank you. You can have the rest for the hour, if you're paying well. Every inch.

So help yourself, darling.

Fine. If you just want to see them, I'm not gonna argue. It all costs the same.

You want to hear 'bout the first one? Fine. I can tell you. It comes from a father. Not mine. This isn't gonna be one of "those" stories, I promise. He was a man who come in here once or twice before I took notice. Always sad-looking in the eyes. More so than most. Had a nervous mouth, always rolled up inside itself. He never came to me, but I'd seen him walk in plenty of times—only to walk right back out once the deed was done. He never looked his girl in the eye, I heard. Most men got too much shame to touch you like that, but this one was exceptional with the distance. For working a feat that you'd think would only bring you closer to somebody else, he could've been miles away. Turned out to be a widower. The way I heard it—he was in the middle of his mount when he just broke out crying, sobbing away on top of his girl. That's what she told all of us afterwards. Never stopped, she said. He just kept on at her, tears falling all over herself. Like he had to get through it. Forcing himself or something. When he finished, she said it was like there wasn't anything left in him. No spirit, none of that manliness. Just enough shame to tell her why. He collapses right on top of her, sobbing-like on her breast—warming her chest up with his story.

None of us take any pity on these men. But every time he come in after I heard that, I couldn't help but feel sorry for him. Can't remember what his wife passed away from. He'd told the girl, I know that. Something you catch and never get rid of. I remember that much. Leaves your lungs all gummy, drowning off your own breath. You cough your life right out.

From what his girl told me, she had to take him in real soft-like. Get him on the unaware, and soothe him the whole way through. Whenever he walked in, it was always to the same lady. But I couldn't help but wish to take him in myself, even if it was only in my mind. I was a clean woman all over back then. No knives had found me yet. Still, most of my men were rougher than most. Heavier than most. They'd all gut me whether I'd allow it or not. Heaving themselves around, like they couldn't hear me rip. So I'd think of that man two rooms over, crying on top of his girl. I'd be taking it in the rear, imagining those tears falling all over me. He was my favorite. Somedays, he'd be my only customer. He'd come in and come in, taking the place of all these other men. It was just a matter of closing the shades. Hearing him say hello and wiping away that first tear.

His girl caught on to my curiousness. I'd go up to her as soon as he was out the door, asking her all kinds of questions. Of course she got tired of telling me the same thing over and over, but I wanted to hear about it. I knew I'd never get him in here, inside of me or any of that. I just knew. If he walked in and his girl was on holiday, he'd just ask for when she'd be coming back and head out himself. The man never dipped into any other. You got to respect that. It was hard to fight off the temptation to walk up to him on a day when she wasn't around. I wanted to offer myself up for a change, hoping he'd be needing it so bad he wouldn't be able to wait for her. One day, I did. I knew his girl would be out for the afternoon, so I waited. Waited through so many men. Passing up good money. I had men chewing off my ear the entire time, telling me to stop lounging 'round, get myself up to my room. Scolding me like I was a child or something.

When he finally stumbled in, I almost leaped on top of that man right there. We all see him come through the front door, but I beat out all of the other girls. He was one to catch, for sure. All of us knew that. But I was up on him before most girls had even checked their breath for cum.

Took a couple quick turns to catch his eye. Even when I did, I didn't keep it for long. But I just kept smiling, telling him my name, how I was a friend of his girl. He asked if she was here, looking over my shoulder in hopes of finding her. All I could think of to say was, "Sorry, sir—but she wanted me to sit in this time."

'Course it was a lie. She never wanted to give that man up to any other. You find a fellow that's going to pay as well as he did, and treat you right ("Nearly like I was the God-damned Queen of England," she'd say), then you'd be a fool to let him go. She never broke a sweat from that man. He was more harmless than mounting an eighty-year-old. Sure he was prize. But I saw him for more than just that. His money wasn't what I was after. I'd even have been fine with a little sweat, even a little rough-and-tumble, if he had it in-side of himself.

I just wanted him in my room. I wanted to hold him.

He gave me his attention on that one. Looked like I'd broken his heart. Didn't say a thing to me. His lip took leave, curling up under itself. The man just up and turned around. Walked out that door with enough speed for me to think he was never coming back. When his girl found out what I'd done, she handed me a couple slaps for letting him go. Right over the face on every one. Not that I blamed her. I was going to miss him, too.

A few months slipped by. I don't know how many. No point in counting here. We're better off letting the days roll right on into each other. Lets us forget how long we've been here. How long we stay. That way, if one of us ever walks out of this place, there's no way we could tally up how much time was lost. But it'd been a while since that man had last come in here. I think his girl even forgot about him. I couldn't. I might have lost sight of some of his features—what his nose looked like or the color of his eyes or things like such. But he was still rolling 'round in my memory. The important parts of him, at least. Had to hold on to him, somehow.

I'd just come out with this hog who loved his spankings, thinking to myself I'd never find me a man who'd keep his pants on for at least five minutes after saying hello. Had to take my dear time to sit myself down, my rear ringing out in prickles and stings. Felt like I'd just sucked up a cactus through my ass. And an hour went by. I just couldn't stand up. Nothing in me wanted to. Not for the likes of any of these men, no. I swear, I felt like crying. But for what? What would I want to cry to them for? If they see a hole big enough for something to come spouting out of me, they're gonna try their damnedest to squeeze a little something of their own back inside. That's all these men are after. Just another hole to bury themselves in.

Not you, darling. I swear. I like you, I do.

I must have been staring off for I don't know how long, 'cause I only come back when I felt this hand touch my shoulder. Not from one of the girls. But from him. I thought I was imagining things again, since he'd never come near me before. I almost paid him no mind, thinking he'd vanish into my head if I tried talking to him. But he just up and talked to me. Asked if I was feeling all right.

I said, yeah.

Asked if I was still working.

I said, sure.

His hands slip behind his back, almost like he was going to pull out a surprise for me or something. Bring me flowers. Instead, up shuffles his son. Looked exactly like his father, so I knew. Couldn't be any older than fifteen years. Had himself a mop of hair that wanted to hide his eyes, but I knew what they looked like. He even had his dad's mouth, only smaller. Less wrinkles than his old man. And pink. Soft, I was sure. He wasn't about to smile, but I did anyways. Holding out my hand with a, "well hello there how d'you do?" I'd never seen a boy go so red before. Looked as if his blood rushed all up into his cheeks. Bit his bottom lip so hard, I was afraid it was going to bleed. He was even quieter than his dad, which I didn't think was possible. Lord knows what they talked like on their own. I couldn't imagine.

No, I could. I wanted to. And I did.

Getting all business-like, his father hands him a roll of bills, tied together like a present. He turns to me, a hand on his boy to hold him in place, making sure he don't run off anywhere, and says something like, "Take care of him, now."

My smile just went wider. Warmer. I think I blushed myself.

And what 'bout you, sir? I asked.

He pulled another one of his silences, eyes running all over.

"I'll wait, thank you."

I took his boy up to my room, holding more of his sweat than his hand. He tried to slip out of my fingers, but I held on to him tight. He was wet all over. Soaking his shirt right through, he was so nervous. I could tell the smell to him was different than any of these other men. I'd been used to a leather scent, something that would wear your nose down until you couldn't help but smell it everywhere you went. Their sweat could right as well have been mine, I soaked up so much of it. But for him, it felt like it was his first time to perspire. Like I'd broken this heat out of him. I kept breathing in through my nose, heavier and heavier with every step, thinking I'd never get a hold of this smell again. The boy was fresh, that's for sure. I didn't know how to handle myself. My thighs were warming up to the idea. I don't want to say I was excited by it all. But I was. Not in a normal way. I was wet for other reasons. It felt like he was answering to different parts of my body.

Fifteen years old. He could have been my boy.

He gave this jump when I closed the door behind him, turning to me like he thought I was about to pounce. Defending himself-like. I just smiled, thinking this is gonna be my crowning achievement. I don't think I'd ever been a first for anyone who came into this place. I couldn't help but see all the responsibility in it. Sounds funny when you talk about it like this. I was gonna be the one to take his boyhood away, slip that manliness in its place. I was gonna have the weight of fifteen years on top of me. Never had anything so small, someone so young to take through. And of all people. I almost felt blessed for the opportunity.

You find pride in these things, no matter what. You learn how to let it fill up your life.

What's your name, boy? I asked him, all sweet-like. Thinking the softer I was, the more he'd just ease up to it. To me.

"Thomas, ma'am," he mumbled back. I'd moved over to the bed while he kept next to the door.

Thomas. That's a strong name. I like it.

"Thank you, ma'am."

You want to come sit next to me, Thomas?

"I don't know, ma'am."

What's with all of this ma'am stuff? Making me feel all old here, Thomas. What'd you take me for? School teacher?

"I apologize. I was just brought up that way, ma'am. That's all."

There was a lightness growing in me. I could feel it in my knees. Men twice his age and twice his size had come into this room and laid all their weight on me, until I thought I'd never be able to stand again. But I'd hold myself up in those moments. Take it like I was stronger than them. And here he was, fifteen years old. Calling me ma'am. Couldn't remember the last time someone called me ma'am.

Well, I said. Whoever taught you those manners should be proud.

His face went white. All of that red he'd been warming me over with rushed right on out.

You all right, darling? I asked.

"My momma taught me."

I could tell it was hard enough for him to say it. Nothing inside him seemed to want to bring the words out of his mouth. They had been dry, all parched on his lips. But once he said it, there were those tears. Slicking up everything. I'd never seen them before in my life. Only heard of them. Imagined them on me for months, washing off all this dry sweat I had covering me. And he had 'em. His father had given them to him. Passed everything down to his son, from his eyes to his mouth. Right on down to his crying.

Looked as if he was about to fall over. I stood up and

grabbed him, bringing him back to my bed. For the first time, he'd let go of all that tenseness inside himself, letting me hold on to him. I laid him down like a set of clothes, he was so limp to me. And crying, just like a boy should. First thing I come up to was his ear, calming him down with my breath, whispering *it's okay, it's okay.* His neck trembled under the words, but I kept whispering *it's okay, it's okay.*

And then something happened within me. Something I've tried to make sense of, but can't really. I kept right next to his ear, saying over and over again, *Momma's here, son. Momma's here,* until there wasn't any space between my lips and his heart, whispering right on inside of him, *It's okay, son. It's okay. Momma's here.*

I managed to pull the sheets out from under him, tucking him in while I lay at his side. I took that boy into my arms, his head nestling right into my neck. His chin rested on my shoulder and I got his mop of hair all over my face. Spent the hour there, just like that. The two of us. Me stroking his hair and him warming up my neck. I didn't know what else to do. Just held him. I kept a hand at his waist while the other took every tear he gave me.

Any talking between us wasn't, really. Not me, at least. It was between him and his mother. The shades were closed shut, so the room could have been any room. It wasn't mine. Not for him. He never saw me in there. I never touched him. He got to say everything he had wanted to, and I'd just keep stroking his hair, stroking his cheek, whispering, *Yes, son. Yes.*

Slowly, almost when there was no time left, his own hands came out from under him—wherever they'd been hiding. They rushed over my stomach and formed a ring around me, until he was hugging me so tight I'd thought I'd cry.

Yeah. After a while, it was hard to tell whose tears was whose.

And we lay there for another hour or so, holding each other just like that.

Mother and son.

When he left, I felt like I was watching my own child head out into the world. Couldn't help but feel proud of myself. Never came in once. But it felt like there was a weight to my belly that had never been there before. It gave me a new strength, something to shield me from of all these other men. No matter how deep they'd drive into me, Thomas would be there, 'cause he had been there, and the feeling of him would stay there for as long as I could be his momma. He'd hold back the sting coming from all these pricks, giving me something to hold on to.

I had the whole day to feel like this. After Thomas and his father left, I stayed behind, still rearing my ass for who-ever'd pay. But I wasn't there. The next day, I come in feeling rejuvenated. Cleansed even, if you'd believe me. Ready to take on anything. One girl tells me I've got a man waiting upstairs for me already. And here it is, not even the end of the morning. It was gonna be a good day.

I walk in here only to find my bed empty, the shades closed. I think whoever the man was, he couldn't wait any longer and gone run himself into another girl's room. Then the door closed behind me. I get some firm hands wrapping around my throat. Before I can even try to breathe, my face is buried into my sheets. These hands work themselves to the back of my head, pushing me deeper into the blankets—until my lower jaw nearly jammed itself back into my throat. I've got my own hands free to swing behind me, finding a man back there. No surprise. He's not built for much, I can tell, but he's angry—giving himself all the strength he needs to keep me in place. I'm clawing away at anything that comes near, my arms having to bend themselves so far backwards, I thought they were going to pop right out. All I can scratch at is the air. He's pushed himself up so close to my ass that I can feel him through his own pants. No surprise.

By now, I'm losing sight of myself. In the dark there, I start seeing colors that I shouldn't be—my head feeling all light. I can just barely hear him yelling at me, hollering like no man has ever done.

"What do you think you are?! What do you think you are?" And what comes along with it all is his belt, his pants. My dress finds itself over my ears, making it all the more hard for me to hear him. But it's coming in clear.

"What do you think you are?" Over and over again, coming right along with his hips. I'm fighting him off at first, watching fireworks explode right in my eyes. I'm feeling bursts all over. Everywhere inside of me. When it feels like I couldn't go any deeper into that bed without ripping my cheeks, I pinch my ass like a vise and twist over onto my back. Lord knows where I found the strength to do that. But it was in me. Always had it in me.

And I find him. In me. He's as scared as I am, looking each other in the eye. Watching that nervous mouth twitch. Those eyes water up.

He finally come into my room.

"What do you think you are?" he whispers. And wouldn't you've guessed it, but here comes those tears. He kept on top of me, repeating himself. He started up again— yelling, grinding, crying. And I took those tears. Collected like broken pieces of china.

It's my fault, I said to myself. *I'll pick it up, I promise. My fault, my fault.*

There wasn't anything to fight against. I eased up and took him. Only struggle I gave was in watching him, staring him right in the eye the whole time. And all of sudden, I get to thinking of Thomas again. Made me ask myself if this is how it happened fifteen years ago. Maybe I could have been his momma, after all.

He pulled away when he finished, still fuming in the head. He wanted more, I could tell. I wanted to reach out for him, hold him and comfort him until that anger went away. But he started pacing the room, muttering to himself. I had my hands up, my elbows bent. Looked like I was hugging the air. I was trying to touch him, but he wouldn't stand still long enough. I couldn't even focus, he was walking 'round so fast. The only thing there was to hold on to was his words, but after a while—what was there to listen to anymore?

What did I think I was, anyway?

Drifted off. Finally. Room was so dark it was easy enough. But I could tell he didn't want me to go just yet. He got back up on top of me, staring me down right in the face. What he left me with was simple to remember. Felt like a dream. But that knife held enough light to catch my eye. Wake me up a little.

"You got no right doing that to my son. To any boy. You

remember that. You play house with someone who pays for it. You hear me, whore? You play mother with someone who asks for it. Not with someone who's trying to push on . . ."

I couldn't keep with him. I tried, but the words just kept getting heavier and heavier. And soon enough, I was gone.

His old girl was the one to find me. She'd been rocking me 'round for I don't know how long. When I come to, first thing I ask her is how she gone and hurt herself. She looks like she don't know what I mean, so I just up and shake my head, saying, "Well, look at you. Got blood all over yourself."

Even when I healed, there was no hiding that scar. Took to my thigh like a birthmark. Stretch mark, maybe? What do they look like? This one had a curve to it. Had myself a moon rising up from my legs, all crescent and white. Looked just like what you see up in the sky, only in between my thighs. Like I'd given birth to a solar system or something.

That man could've buried his blade elsewhere, I know. There are worser places, which makes me think he still had some of that . . . compassion in him, I guess. He could've gone for the belly. Hell, right for my heart. Talk about a caring man.

I asked for the others. Carving up all the places he should've gone. First man to take me found that scar mighty quick, almost was frightened by it. So I took to him, almost motherly-like, saying, "It's okay, it's okay. Want one you can call your own?" I bought myself a knife out of my own pay, after that. Most of us keep one for our protection. I keep mine for my men. Got it under my pillow, right now. Hold on, let me show you.

Now I have a sun scabbing at my back, enough stars

scarring up my arms to light this entire room. I got a galaxy all to my own, here. Planets I name after my men, giving each of them a home of their own, where they can bury their pain with their blades. Offer any of these greedy boys the chance, and they'll take it. All they're after is someone who's gonna care enough to give them a place to dig.

I'm up for it. Need to be. I come into this room and I want that boy with me again, one way or another. His tears fell over me like shooting stars drifting across my body. They soaked into my skin—and look what I got now, because of it. A cosmos all of my own, a heavenly body you're only gonna see once you lay down your money.

Here it is. Sharp one, isn't it? Take it. Don't even worry about the extra dollar. Just take it. Please. Find a spot and take it.

That boy's got to be with me, please. Please.

Thank you.

Thank you.

rodeo inferno

You hear that? Under all the cheering. Something's hiding out there, waiting for us in that stadium. I can feel it. Just below the applause. If I listen hard enough, I can almost make it out. I got to train my ears to stop hearing those hands. Get underneath the uproar and I'll find just what it is that we're dealing with here.

It's big, I know that. With so many people rooting it on, it's got to be.

See? You hear that? They're praising the damn thing, the whole crowd. Egging it to stomp on the ground, my God. What have we gotten ourselves into? I don't know about you, but I hear hooves digging into the dirt.

I get the feeling we're in the middle of some sacrilege here.

I'm sorry, but they are not paying us enough to do this. I'm not so sure if I want to go through with it, anymore. For twenty bucks, I'd much rather take the head off a chicken with my own teeth than step out into that stadium.

I mean, look at you. What kind of outfit do you call that? I'm not seeing anything funny about it. No one's going to laugh at a clown that can't even keep his wig on straight. And you're already sweating your makeup off. Your face is so slippery, you look like you're on the other end of a puddle that keeps getting stepped in. I can't even focus on your features from two feet in front of you, for Christ's sake. Some poor kid's going to think your face is melting away, all 'cause you can't keep from overheating underneath that red mop of hair you got now. And from the way you're wearing it, you look like your whole head is about to slump off.

Clowns, they said. *We need clowns.*

Tell me, what's so funny about us?

These pants have got enough holes in them to make me think they've been chewed on. And with holes the size of these, I don't want to see the mouth that made them. If that's what's waiting for us outside, then no thank you. I got an offer down at the county fair for a dollar for every chicken head I swallow. But I have never heard anyone say I'd make a good clown. *Look* at me. They can't even give me a clean costume, for Christ's sake. I mean, what is this? That's not blood, is it? These have got to be dirt stains, right?

Then why are my pants all covered in them?

They're thinking, since we all live on the train tracks, they can just pluck up as many of us as they need. I've seen these people come around, looking for help. *Help,* they call it. Jesus. *Twenty bucks for a good day's work,* they say. But you never see the fellow again. I never have. These people come through, wearing their ten-gallon hats and fancy rhinestone jackets. Got them cowboy boots all polished, belt buckles shining right in your eye—I'd bet they're trying to hypnotize you. *We're looking for some help,* they say. *Come on down to the rodeo and we'll set you up with a king's wage.*

Yeah, they know how to pluck a man. Promise him a king's wage. But for what? Dressing him up like a dirty fool. You got men disappearing from the train tracks every weekend, just after these people mosey through *looking for some help.* Well, I tell you, my friend—I'm going to get to the bottom of all this. I don't care how deep into the bullshit I go, I'm going to find out what we stepped in, here.

And hell. If I can pocket twenty bucks at the same time, then I guess it isn't such a bad day, now—is it?

Hold up.

You had to've heard that. You did, didn't you? Come on, now! Don't tell me I'm all alone on this. How liquored up did they get you? Jesus! You got whiskey dribble washing the makeup off your chin! Snap back to me, here. Don't you see? That's what these people are hoping for. The slower your senses, the quicker that thing out there is going to drive into you. And it will rip you to pieces. I know it.

Just listen for a change. Can you hear it breathing out there? It's got to have nostrils the size of my mouth when I open wide, two times over. And after wrapping my lips around enough chicken heads to whip me up a gullet the girth of a Firestone tire, you better believe I'm talking big here. *Huge.* And I'm only on its nose, now. No, I'm thinking it's got to be evil all over. Nose. Hooves. Want to make a bet it's got some horns on it? How about a tail? You want to guess what color it is?

How about red?

We got some idol-worship on our hands here, my friend. We're sitting outside a Black Mass going on, right now. You'd be blind to it all by now, if you weren't already so drunk off of that rotgut they fed you. Don't you see? We sold our soul for twenty dollars. Do you need it any clearer for you?

Well, how about this. A week ago, I'd been down at the fair, tearing off anywhere from ten, twenty chicken heads an hour. I was making myself some good money. I took a break to cough up a few loose feathers, sitting back behind some trailers close to the rodeo. My throat was a little sore from all that chicken kickback. (That's a technical term we use, when your teeth first find the spine, slipping in between the two vertebrae of your choice. In biting, that neck's going to take its last spasm, and take it hard. You got to worry over the chicken kicking back its beak into your throat—either driving down into your Adam's apple or reaching back for your

own bone.) I had been going at it for so long that day, that I
had started to tire. I wasn't snapping fast enough, giving
them chickens enough nerve to snap back. So I needed a few
minutes to heal. At least get my second wind.

But before I knew it, sleep came on. Took me by the
hand and walked me off into a dream. Where I was sipping
from a freshly opened bottle of whiskey. I was taking heavy
slugs, until it didn't matter where the whiskey went—just as
long as it was running over my body. It cleansed the chicken
blood from my chin. The stray feathers washed away in a
flood of alcohol.

But sweet dreams quickly sour when you sleep this
close to the unholy rodeo. I was brought back to the parking
lot by a sound of men dragging along something heavy. I
wouldn't have paid it much mind, hadn't it been for the fact
that what they were throwing away was still alive. It was one
of these fools, dressed just like you and me. He was moaning
low as those men stripped him down, taking off his clothes
and leaving him for dead, naked. I waited until I knew they
were gone, creeping over to him—only to find what was left
wasn't much to look at, at all. The poor fellow had enough
holes in him to hold every finger I had. He had the makeup
on, face painted white with a big red smile. But even underneath all that lively color, I could see his soul slipping away.
It was happening right before my eyes. To see a husk looking
so happy, when the insides are bleeding through every
hole—I couldn't keep my meal down. One look at this clown
and I had him wrapped in chicken salad. Practically tarred
and feathered the poor fellow myself.

But somehow, my sickness must have been of some sustenance to him. I can't explain it. The whiskey and chicken-neck upchuck got his eyes to widen, blessing him with one more breath to live by. And with it, he grabs me by the shoulder, tight, making sure I'm following his other hand. He's pointing to his wounds, placing a finger at the lowest hole and poking at it. Up comes enough blood for him to paint with. I watch him while he connects one hole to the next, a red line fastening the two punctures together. From there, he crosses over his chest, reaching a rip just above his nipple. And so on and so forth, zigzagging across his body.

Once he finished, he took my hand and held it hard, mustering up what little strength he had left to shake me. To make me see the *pentagram* gored into his body! With his last exhale, he whispered to me in some foreign tongue that I took to be Latin, or whatever these priests speak when exorcising Satan—

"...*diablo de bullo*..."

When his hands let me go, he left me with a responsibility to my fellow man. Evil is in our midst. Evil waits for us out in that stadium, and I have heard its name. It is spoken by the damned, the clowns of this world. I've even heard it over the loud-speaker outside. They say we're in store for a great show at the rodeo today. From the sound of the crowd, I'd say, he's hungry for us already.

You hear that?

They're trying to hide it with their clapping, but I'm not fooled. He's out there, waiting for you and me. Kicking up enough dirt to disappear, only to drive right into you when you least expect it. And the crowd is going to watch on, see you take it with a big painted smile on your face, thinking you're thankful for what's been done. Just like the fool they knew you were for taking this job.

Me, I'm prepared. I'm taking this devil by the horns and fighting him with a little bit of his own medicine. I figure, as I walk through the stadium of death, the chickens will be my angels—their heavenly wings outspread in my stomach to protect me. My saving grace is in my gut, with enough beaks in my belly to kick back at anything that comes charging. One poke into me and I'll pop in a powder keg of poultry!

I wear these rags knowing quite well who's worn them before. And today, I'm standing up for them all. Every last lost soul.

No one's laughing at this clown. No.

Today, they're all going to see just how far twenty bucks can really go.

it goes rickety

I, Stanley Farmer, had built the mouth that led straight to hell—and then charged people fifty cents for the trip down.

I'd be the first to tell you: from my very own God-damned hands that ride came around. And I promise you, it would never've stopped spinning as long as I had one hand to work with. Because that is just what that man-made cyclone did—come around and come around, again and again, at sixty miles an hour. A bucket of sorts, nailed together with wood and springs—*Hell's Gate* was the one ride you never went on twice. The damnation you went through with your stomach alone taught a lesson never to be shaken. That, if there ever was a hell on earth, you were pinned up inside it right now—without a hope of ever getting out. Just when you thought it couldn't get any worse, a squeeze from a rusty lever and I'd send the gears into a frenzy, spitting the laws of gravity out through the top . . . *as the floor dropped out from beneath your feet*, leaving nothing in between the two but frantic air.

After forty-three years of traveling up and down the county fair circuit, I tell you—it was getting hard to tell where my hands stopped and the levers started. If there ever was a case of man marrying machine, here's where it was.

'Cause here's where it goes rickety, my friends. The sound of my own career winding down all started when this father wanted to take his two tykes for a spin—one of his little boys passing under the height of my belt. A rule for riding was you always had to come up over *ol' Stanley's pants*. Anyone lower than my crotch might end up two states over. But this father, extra-generous with the price of admission, slipped me this wink, saying, "Oh, come on pal. I don't see anyone else cutting in line to get on."

I just licked my extra quarter and grinned.

Stepping inside the Gate, this father got his first wind of some second thoughts. In comes my rusty voice from a speaker overhead, crackling out the orders to "Get ready for the ride of your life!" And before anyone could breathe, a set

of hidden hydraulics started to groan, the Gate rocking itself
to life. Gravity gave this father's back nowhere else to go but
up against the wall—his sons at his sides, each clinging to
the leg of their choice. Only an angel could've blessed those
boys with enough breath to holler, but when the Gate's floor
dropped and those three stayed up—*out it came*, two howls at
each side of this father flopping around like he was some fish
thrown up against the wall . . .

Yeah, well. Sniffing out the ruckus quicker than a dog
to its own rear end, Wasco Hellman Jr., proud owner and
proprietor of the Hellman county fair, lifted his attention up
to a wave of wet sounds. A lump of chaw buried behind his
bottom lip, a cup of old cola in his one good hand for spitting—these were his bare necessities for travel. And today,
Wasco found himself nearly *propelled* to all the commotion,
his feet knowing clearly well where to go.

Greeted by the sight of these two boys yellowing their
pants, he found his feet in a fresh puddle of pee-pee—the
leather in his shoes softening.

"What in the hell is going on here, Stanley?" Wasco
asked. "You got two kids watering the grass, and one guy
dizzier than a dust devil!"

Hell, it was true. That father had started shuffling towards the hot dog vendor, only to spin around the opposite
way—trying to walk in *three* different directions at once.
With his boys jumping on at his waist, they all hitched a ride
the rest of the way out of the fair, a golden exhaust of kiddy-
piss trailing close behind.

Wasco just spit. "You want to explain to me why it is

every time I get complaints, they always got to do with you and this ride?" He started in on me, working his chops up into a frenzy—chewing me out. Saying things like, people come here to have fun, not puke up their popcorn. Wanting balloons and shit. None of this throw-up. The more Wasco's mouth had at me, the slicker his lips went, wetting themselves up with tobacco spit. I lost track of what he was saying, his words slipping out so fast, I was behind by his second breath. "Times are hard. You know that. *I know that.* I'm having enough trouble making my own ends meet, here— let alone pay everyone else in this place. Now I've been thinking about this for a long, *long* time, and I . . . Shit. I feel like I've given you every chance I got. I don't think I've got any other choice but to shut you down."

Not a sound came out of me but the stretch of skin making two fists—one for each of Wasco's kidneys. Hell, I was more a part of this place than candy apples! Take away the Gate, and this fair would end up lopsided from too much fun. If people were looking for a ride that was going to take their minds off of their troubles for a while, well, I had just that. The Gate whisked your worries way, flushing 'em right out from your skull. Every fair needs an asshole, that one ride kids would only step on if they'd been dared to. And damn right, that was me.

I heard a hum of engine parts all around me, the momentum building up so much in my mind, my arms wanted to start whirly-gigging on Wasco. His chin glistened with chaw, the sun caught in these brown rivers running right down his neck. I could've knocked that lower jaw off with one swing, sending it into the air like I was playing a game of horseshoes. Wrap it around a tent spike and score on my first punch. He saw it in me, too—his eyes squirming in their sockets, looking for an escape. Walking backwards with his one good hand in the air, Wasco waved his cup in a hurried goodbye—a trickle of chaw running down his arm. A final spit to the ground and he was gone.

The Gate and me were left standing in the heart of the fair, the two of us clotting up the flow of people passing by. A burning sensation suddenly stretched over my heart as if my chest hairs had caught on fire. It thinned out the blood fueling my body, the turns of this ticker slowing down to a limp thump. If the Gate wouldn't budge, neither would my heart.

So the mind that held itself inside my skull started to spin on its stem, my thoughts pinned up against the flat of my cranium. A point had to be made. A sharp one. Something that'd have ringleaders from all over barking for years to come. Well, quicker than you can say timber, there popped up a plan into my head. The two of us would leave, hell yes. We'd just take our vacation six feet under. A suicide run. *The* suicide run. To dig my own grave and open up a circus for worms was better than giving up the Gate.

I tell you, the thought of it made my mind race—the insides of my head spinning so fast, my skull rattled. The hum of hell was a harmony to my ears. Giving a spit to the Hellman county fair, I looked at the people paying no mind and grinned. My eyes were racing too fast to realize that my sap had landed on a newly found customer. It wasn't until there came a tug at my leg that I noticed, turning around

and looking down to find this boy—plumper than a potato—standing at my crotch.

"Hey mister, you need to get invited to ride this thing?"

A cone-shaped hat on top of his head, a halo of half-
eaten cotton candy sticking to his hair, the boy was covered
in cake crumbs from his cheeks to kneecaps. There, behind
him, were five or six others just like him, bellies covered in
chocolate.

Said the ride had been shut down, grumbling at him to
go give someone else his quarters.

That got the boy sniffling. "If you don't let me and my
friends on, I'm gonna tell my father. And when my father
finds out . . . he's gonna have your blood flavoring his snow
cone."

I took a deep breath, turned back to the kid. Leaned
over so I was right in his face, close enough to lick off that
smear of icing streaked across his nose. "Who's your father,
kid?"

"Oh, you know who he is. He's the one who runs this
shitty place. And that means he runs you, too."

My eyes halted dead in their sockets. Licking my lips
to loosen them up, out came a row of crooked teeth the color
of dried corn kernels. Revenge comes in many shapes and
sizes, you see—and today, well. It was looking like a half-
dozen ten-year-olds.

Graciously stepping out of the way, I beckoned the
birthday boy on inside—proudly introducing Wasco's son to
my own. Fueled on Cracker Jacks and soda pop, the lot of his
pudgy friends followed him through. They giggled at the

jiggle in their bellies, the wooden boards warping underneath their feet. Now, I knew what had to be done. Making a
pact right then and there—father and son shook between
lever and hand, the controls pushed to their hilt. From here
on out, there was no turning back—only turning forwards,
again and again, a thousand times over!

Gritting its metal teeth, the Gate's gears groaned into
motion. Trudging over to the entranceway, I reeled myself
back and gave it a good run and jumped on into the Gate—
just barely making it inside before the door turned into a
blur. Those boys, round by nature, all rolled back into the
wall. Boards began to break, a similar sensation transplanted
into me—the ride and my ribs splintering apart.

But the Gate didn't let up. Every spin was a lap closer
to sickness—a dizzy spell licking away at the backs of those
boys' eyes, the sounds from within their stomachs a song just
waiting to be sung. And there I was in the midst of it all—
my cankers crying out in a chorus of hallelujahs, my teeth
chattering up a racket, cheering, "Geeeet readyyy for the
riiide of yooour liiiiiife!"

And it happened. As the floor dropped out from below
our feet, everything inside that barrel went horribly wet. It
began with the tiniest of belches—just a pinch of air pushing up from the birthday boy himself. Just once around, his
mouth was empty. The next, he was letting go of everything
he had for three meals past. In a choir of upset tummies,
the sick feeling spread from one boy to the next. Bellies
quaked, livers began to shake, and every bite of cake came
back on out. Back were the corn dogs, back was the cotton

candy. In a cheap carny exorcism, there came a whole gush of bilious spirits, rushing out into the whirlpool of air— having nowhere else to land *but back in the face of the boy who let it go.*

But the ride wasn't over yet. I took one final breath and turned myself over face-first onto the Gate. Sinking my teeth into the soft wood, I bit down on the boards—until the splinters nestled in my gums, fastening the two of us together. There were a few more laps around before I let my own rectum open wide, the soil in my pants spackling as many cracks in the wood as it could. No butts about it, I was going to drill the world a new asshole—flushing the fair straight down to hell.

The blood in my body had nowhere else to run but up inside my skull. The swell left me with a warm feeling all over, the vessels inside my head going off like popcorn in a pan. If the muscles in my lips hadn't given way, I would've smiled—my jaw splitting open over the wood in a welcoming embrace. Because what I saw would've made any father proud. After waiting a total of forty-some years, my hell had finally come around. And around. And around. And around. And around and around and around and around and around and around and around and around and around and around and around and around and around and around and round it goes, where it stops, nobody knows . . .